"Are your sea legs failing you?"

Camille's face had a hint of a smile.

Maddox swallowed. "Just off balance for a minute."

He didn't need to explain why. The flush that came to her cheeks right before she spun and headed for the door told him she understood what had put him off-kilter. Would they have a chance to be alone or even talk any time soon?

"Are we ever going to talk about it?" he asked right before she got to the door.

She stopped but didn't turn back. If he could only see her eyes, her expression...

"Is there anything new to say?" she asked, her voice a low neutral.

"A lot has changed."

She shook her head. "You can't change the past."

With those words, she walked down the steps.

No, he couldn't change the past. All he could do was build a future for his son and himself.

Dear Reader,

Home for the Holidays is the second book in the Return to Christmas Island series, and it has all my favorite things: romance, Christmas, a wedding, homemade candy, an island and a second chance at love.

Christmas Island is in the Great Lakes region of the United States. Just off the Michigan shoreline, it has warm summers and snowy winters. It's a beautiful area with clear water, trees and rocky shores. Several hundred people live on the island all year, but Christmas Island really comes alive for the summer tourist crowd and the holidays. Day visitors travel aboard the ferry to the island, where they bike, rent golf carts, shop in downtown boutiques, enjoy the scenery and buy souvenirs of their excursion.

In *Home for the Holidays*, Camille Peterson comes back to Christmas Island after a seven-year absence. Her high school sweetheart broke her heart at the end of senior year, and she thought she'd never return. She also thought there wouldn't be a second chance for her and Maddox May, but you never know what magic can happen on an island where it's always the most wonderful time of the year.

I hope you'll love your visit to Christmas Island and come back for the rest of the series!

Happy reading,

Amie Denman

HEARTWARMING

Home for the Holidays

—

Amie Denman

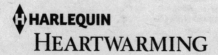

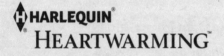

ISBN-13: 978-1-335-42661-1

Home for the Holidays

Copyright © 2022 by Amie Denman

Recycling programs for this product may not exist in your area.

This edition published by arrangement with Harlequin Books S.A.

For questions and comments about the quality of this book, please contact us at CustomerService@Harlequin.com.

Harlequin Enterprises ULC
22 Adelaide St. West, 41st Floor
Toronto, Ontario M5H 4E3, Canada
www.Harlequin.com

Printed in U.S.A.

Amie Denman is the author of forty contemporary romances full of humor and heart. A devoted traveler whose parents always kept a suitcase packed, she loves reading and writing books you could take on vacation. Amie believes everything is fun, especially wedding cake, roller coasters and falling in love.

Visit the Author Profile page
at Harlequin.com for more titles.

CHAPTER ONE

THE SIGN IN front of the Christmas Island School said it all: Welcome Home. Camille Peterson had only been back inside the school once since her high school graduation, for her younger sister's commencement ceremony. When she'd left the island seven years earlier, she'd had no intention of returning. But she'd chosen to come home after all, where memories were as thick as the fudge in her family's candy store. Indulging in those memories was sweet up to a point, but too much left her feeling queasy.

"This is so much fun, all three of us together going to the school reunion," Chloe said as she put her arms around Camille and Cara and took a selfie of the three of them in front of the school's sign. Like everything else on the island, the school's colors reflected the holiday theme—red and green with a reindeer for a mascot. "I'm framing this picture," Chloe added.

Camille's younger sister, Cara, shot her a look with a raised eyebrow and grin that pretty much said what they both knew about their oldest sister. Chloe was the sappy, sentimental one of the group, a total sucker for family heirlooms, island traditions and preserving flowers. Camille's homecoming corsage was probably in a box somewhere at her parents' house, but she had no intention of lifting that lid.

"Can we leave early if people start hugging and talking about how great high school was?" Cara asked.

Camille laughed. "I'm pretty sure that's the point of reunions. No matter how we felt about school at the time, it's a beautiful rainbow of memories now."

Chloe frowned. "But it was beautiful. Everything about Christmas Island is magical."

Camille noticed her older sister's shiny eyes and guessed what was coming.

"Maybe I'm making a mistake by getting married and leaving the island," Chloe said. She clutched Camille's arm. "Do you think it's a mistake? I mean, you left right after high school, but then you finally came back. Do you regret leaving?"

Laughter from inside the school's gymnasium drifted out to them. Camille hadn't wanted to come to the reunion and relive her high school days. Just thinking about the graduation ceremony where she'd smiled through a broken heart made her want to run back home. Except home on the island included her childhood bedroom, which looked the same as it had when she'd left for college. The ruffled pink bedspread and the hand-me-down dresser her mother had painted in cheerful colors to match the candy-colored curtains were still there, along with her ice skates and favorite childhood books.

If she was really going to stay on Christmas Island for good, she needed to get her own place. Camille made a mental note to look for a downtown apartment, perhaps one of the places over a storefront. She could feel better about her independence, even if she was taking over the management of her family's business, if she went home to her own place without candy colors everywhere. Perhaps a nice gray color palette, she thought. Furniture and rugs in muted earth tones.

"Coming back was my choice," Camille assured her sister Chloe. "And marrying Dan is your choice. You're going to be perfectly happy on the mainland, and we'll promise to make a big fuss over you whenever you come back to visit."

"I'll name one of my barn cats after you so I won't forget you," Cara added.

Instead of letting any tears slip down her cheeks, Chloe patted her eyes with a tissue and smiled. "Well, then, let's party like we're back in high school." She linked arms with Camille and Cara and marched them toward the gymnasium's door.

Camille put on a brave face for her sisters' sake. They were allowed happy memories, and she wouldn't take that away from them. Leaving had allowed her to force her feelings into a box. In the past seven years, Camille had come home only for important family occasions, and each time she'd visited Christmas Island, she'd looked over her shoulder, wondering when she was going to run into him.

She was back, but she was moving forward. And that meant controlling the crushing feeling around her heart whenever she saw Maddox May. She had to stop checking the rearview mirror for obstacles.

Would Maddox come to the all-class reunion? Would he expect to see her there? Both answers were probably yes. Everyone who'd graduated from the small island school came to reunions if they were in the area, and Maddox still lived and worked on the island. His circumstances had drastically changed, but that didn't alter the mistakes he'd made in the past.

"Here we go," Cara whispered to her. "I'm sticking to you like glue."

"Thank you," Camille said, her chest tight at the thought of Maddox's betrayal.

"It's a beautiful evening, and they have picnic tables set up outside the back entrance of the gym. We can escape out there," Cara said.

Camille smiled. Her younger sister was the perfect opposite to her older one. Chloe loved crowds, while Cara preferred quiet island trails. Camille was always somewhere in the middle. She considered joining a small group of classmates at a table decorated with the school colors, or else getting back on the family golf cart and speeding away. Being in the middle and always seeing both sides of every story had been a useful skill as a history major, but it was also part of the delicate landscape of coming home and navigating relationships.

"Hey," Camille heard someone call. It was Violet, owner of a clothing boutique and the island's fashionista. She waved at them from beneath red and green streamers.

Chloe stopped to look at a display of yearbooks laid out in a long line, and Camille and Cara made their way to Violet's table.

Violet scanned Camille's outfit as she walked over to the table. "Nice. Flattering, but effortless. Perfect blue with your gorgeous blond hair."

Camille laughed. "It was the only thing in Chloe's closet that wasn't a pastel color. Borrowing clothes from my sister is one of the fun things about moving back home."

Violet made room for Camille and Cara on her bench seat. Camille was sure these were the same tables that had been rolled into and out of the gym to serve school lunch when she'd gone to school here. She pushed away the memory of waiting for a special someone to walk through the gym doors for lunch every day. Even if Maddox showed up now, there was an ocean of water under the bridge for them. Ice-cold water.

"Your sister Chloe might need a new wardrobe for her life on the mainland. Being a candy girl is great here on Christmas Island, but it might have limitations elsewhere," Violet said with a smile. "I could help her out if she comes by my shop. I have some beautiful fall colors in stock."

Camille laughed. She'd gone through a time in junior high when she resented being called a candy girl. Her family owned a thriving candy and fudge business on Christmas Island, and her childhood memories were wrapped in the sensory experience of kitchen heat and chocolate aromas. The three Peterson daughters somehow became known as the candy girls, especially when their mother dressed them in colors that made them look like gumdrops. When

Camille left the island for college, she'd started dressing in gray and black. Finally, her roommate had suggested that Camille try some jewel tones with her blond hair and fair coloring.

Tonight Camille wore a sleeveless sapphire-blue dress with low-heeled black sandals. Looking around the school gym where so much had taken place in Camille's life, she was glad she wore a sophisticated cocktail dress. She wasn't a girl anymore, even if she vividly remembered volleyball practice, study halls, school dances, lunchroom talks with her friends and graduation.

Chloe joined the group and squeezed into a seat next to Camille. "Nothing new," she said, nodding toward the high school friend she'd been chatting with.

"Not surprising, since you just saw her yesterday when she brought her daughter into the candy store," Camille said. At twenty-seven, most of the ten people Chloe had graduated with had partners and families. She'd be joining the married couples soon. Camille's graduating class had a few married members, but at twenty-five, it also included singles like Camille and Violet, not to mention the guy who had once kissed her behind the bleachers.

"If we're very lucky," Cara said, "some island visitors will crash the party and we'll have someone new to talk to instead of the same boys we grew up with."

Violet and Camille nodded, but Chloe shook her head. "That's not the point of a reunion."

Camille snorted. "Every day on this island is a reunion."

"True," Violet said with a laugh. "Just walk down the street or hop on the ferry and boom, you run into someone you know."

Camille winced. She tried not to think about the ferry that served Christmas Island.

Two brothers owned and operated the service, but only one of them had broken her heart right outside on a bench under an oak tree.

"I'll get us drinks," she said. Camille spun around to head for the bar without asking what anyone wanted, and that was when she saw Maddox May entering the gym.

He hadn't changed much. A bit more

filled out since high school, a layer of confidence in the way he moved. She'd seen him a dozen times since she'd returned at the beginning of summer, but somehow seeing him back in the high school setting where they'd fallen in love was a gut punch.

She turned back around, and she knew from her friends' faces that they'd seen Maddox, too.

"I'll come with you," Cara said as she hopped up and smoothed her red dress. "And help carry the drinks." Cara looped an arm around Camille and spoke quietly to her as they walked toward the bar. "We're in the same old place, but you've changed, he's changed, everything has changed. Don't feel weird about it."

Camille nodded and absorbed her younger sister's excellent advice. Her older sister, Chloe, always put drama and romance at the front of the line, so she would probably be advising Camille to rekindle the old flame. The only thing Camille wanted to breathe new life into was her family's business. She'd come home to take it over now that Chloe was leaving, and she was going to transform Island

Candy and Fudge and make its name and products known far beyond the small island where she'd grown up.

She was leaving the past behind her, even if she was back at home in her childhood bedroom. To move into the future, she wouldn't be dwelling on how the business used to be run, and she certainly wouldn't waste a tear on a lost high school love.

MADDOX MAY HAD come to the Christmas Island all-class reunion for only one reason: his brother, Griffin, had made him. The whole town was talking about them, and Griffin thought showing up at gossip central would help dispel the rumors circulating about the brothers' newfound wealth. Everyone knew their aunt had given them millions. Flora Winter wanted to enjoy seeing the May brothers use their inheritance, so she'd given them half of the money along with the deed to her island mansion a few months earlier.

The May brothers had known it wouldn't be long before island talk caught up with their windfall. They'd tried to keep it quiet, but the rapid expansion of their downtown ferry dock had perked up the ears of local gossips. Maddox's ex-wife had also blurted the news to a friend on the island, and the secret had spread like the aroma of fudge mixed with lake air across Christmas Island.

"At least not every single person in the room stared at us when we walked in," Griffin said. "That's good news."

Maddox didn't find that comforting. The one person whose opinion interested him had deliberately turned away when she saw him. Camille Peterson's long blond hair fell down her back and contrasted with her vivid blue dress. She was even more beautiful at twenty-five than she had been at eighteen, when she left the island.

He wished he could recapture their easy friendship...their love...from that time, but she'd been furious with him and had refused to speak to him throughout that summer after they graduated. He'd deserved it, and apologizing hadn't been enough. It probably never would be.

"You should have brought Rebecca," Maddox said. "She always seems to know what to say in awkward situations, and she can probably explain about the money better than we can."

"She's not on the island," Griffin said. "I took her over on the early ferry today."

"I assumed you'd want her here at the reunion with you."

"She's driving to Chicago to clean out her apartment for good and bring her stuff back so she can move into the Winter Palace."

"It's nice that Flora has such faith in her, and we're darn lucky she's going to manage our money for us."

"Very lucky," Griffin acknowledged with a smile.

Maddox was happy for his brother, who'd accidentally found true love mixed in with a massive financial windfall. The summer that had just ended had been tumultuous, but Griffin and Rebecca Browne seemed made for each other. Now Rebecca had one floor of Flora Winter's island mansion all to herself to live in, and she'd been given permission to use the mansion's library as her office. She'd be available with her financial and business knowledge to help them expand their island ferry and hotel business. Griffin would soon be vacating his small downtown apartment and moving into the Winter Palace, too, taking the upper floor with its bedroom, den, luxury bathroom and expansive deck for himself.

Maddox would feel left out if he hadn't inherited their childhood home, which he was already planning to upgrade and expand. He wanted to turn it into a home where his son would have the childhood he deserved. When they were kids, he and his brother had visited the Winter Palace on holidays and special occasions, and his son would grow up doing the same. There was no place on earth with the freedom and safety of Christmas Island.

"So what's our strategy?" Griffin asked. "Splitting up and answering questions honestly without saying more than we have to or just grabbing the microphone and making an announcement?"

Maddox laughed. "And what would you say?"

Griffin scrubbed a hand over his short hair. "Man, I wish Rebecca was here. I've known everyone in this room all my life, but it's weird having this major thing hanging in the air."

Maddox knew exactly what it was like to have something unresolved lingering over him like a cloud. Should he approach Camille directly and make pleasant conversation, as if he hadn't destroyed her trust and then married someone else? He was trying to teach his son to be truthful with himself and others, but laying the truth at Camille's feet seven years ago hadn't bought him any mercy.

A projector flashed images on the far wall of the gym, a row of fluorescent lights turned off to enhance the colors. The cash bar was set up near the slideshow.

Camille was at the bar with her sister Cara, and their backs were to Maddox and Griffin. The image changed from a 1970s graduation picture to a far more recent photo. A picture of students reading a play aloud in English class. He remembered the moment the picture had been taken. He'd read the part of Romeo, and Camille had played Juliet. It was early in their junior year, and they'd been lifelong friends. For a moment, Maddox was right back to being sixteen going on seventeen.

Camille stood across the room, reading from a green textbook. The sunlight streamed in behind her, illuminating her blond hair. Her lines were about the sea and how it was deep and boundless, and his thoughts wandered to the lake outside until he realized Camille was staring at him with a curious expression before she'd quickly glanced back down at the book and delivered her lines about love. "The more I give to thee, the more I have."

She hadn't looked back up from the book, but he'd known those words were for him, not Romeo. He remembered the stark emotion of realizing that he was in love with Camille. Did she remember the shock of that revelation, too? Were those memories tangled up with their reading of the Shakespeare play just as they were tangled with every other high school association for him?

He saw Camille's head turn toward the slideshow and he knew the moment she saw the picture, too. Her shoulders stiffened, and her hands closed and opened as if she were trying to grab hold of something...or else let it go.

He'd ruined the end of their senior year, and he was pretty sure he'd destroyed *Romeo and Juliet* for her, too. The years Camille had lived away from the island had softened his guilt, but having her back to stay meant they had to find a way to reconcile. It was an opportunity he'd never believed he was going to get.

"Drink first?" Griffin asked. "Unless you think it's too crowded at the bar." Griffin nodded toward Camille and Cara Peterson.

"I think it's a good start," Maddox said.

He strode to the bar before he had time to change his mind. He couldn't keep avoiding Camille. They were adults now. Wasn't it time they had an honest conversation about what had happened? It wouldn't change the past, but it might make it easier to live with.

Cara Peterson balanced a tray with four drinks, and Camille was digging through her purse as Maddox walked up.

"I'll buy," Maddox said.

Camille looked up. "No, thank you."

"I want to," he said.

Camille hesitated, and he could almost see her deciding how to handle him. She'd kept him at arm's length all summer and had been just on the cool side of civil when they'd been tossed together in social situations. They hadn't spoken about what happened seven years ago.

Despite his resolve to find a peaceful way to move forward and share the island, Maddox felt a rush of heat around his heart. Maybe it was being back where their first love had begun. Was it possible that his feelings for Camille had gone dormant but had never actually died? Did she feel the same way?

It was too dangerous to think about. He had his son to consider, and playing with fire wouldn't make him a very good role model.

"Is my brother holding up the line?" Griffin asked as he took the tray of drinks from Cara. "I'll carry these for you while Maddox pays."

Before Maddox could object, Griffin walked off with Cara. Cara shot Camille an apologetic glance, and Camille gave her a little nod. Her younger sister was right. Everyone had changed, and that high school betrayal was a long time ago.

Camille hesitated for a moment, as if she was wavering between letting Maddox buy her drinks and being stuck longer alone with him if she handled the transaction for herself.

"Thank you," she said politely in a tone she might use for someone she'd just met. With a glance at the wall where the picture of them as star-crossed lovers had been a moment ago, she turned and walked back to her table without ever looking directly at him.

Griffin returned as the bartender put two glasses on the counter. "I saw Jordan and Mike at a table outside," he said. He picked up his drink and waited for Maddox to follow suit. "We'll start with a friendly crowd where we can practice dodging questions, but I'm kind of glad the cat's out of the bag. There are no secrets on this island," Griffin said.

As Maddox walked past the table where the Peterson sisters sat with Violet and some other friends, he thought about how right his brother was.

CHAPTER TWO

Island Candy and Fudge had a pink-striped awning, pink countertops and the company name spelled out in pink letters with gilt edges on the front window. Huge vinyl stickers depicting lollipops and fudge covered the windows overlooking Holly Street. Every visitor to the island would smell the fudge boiling and see the sign as they walked, biked or enjoyed a ride in a rented golf cart past the store.

At least, that was how it had always been. The Peterson family had allowed people's senses of smell and sight to lead them to the store, where they'd take home pink bags filled with treats. If Camille's plan worked, candy and fudge shoppers wouldn't just be shopping on the island. They would be ordering online or buying Island Candy and Fudge products at select retail outlets all over the region. Camille stood on the front sidewalk and smiled at her reflection in the morning light glancing off the shop windows. Her plan was already taking shape.

"I don't know," Camille's mom, Melinda, said. "We've always been a local commodity. The only place in the world you can get our secret fudge recipe is right here on Christmas Island."

"You could call that exclusive," Camille said. "I think it's limiting."

"Chloe turned down that offer from the internet place a few years ago," Melinda said.

Camille tightened her jaw and looked away from her reflection. She didn't like seeing the frustration on her face caused by the Chloe comparison for the five hundredth time. Daughter number one in the Peterson family had been the first choice for taking over the family business, her passion for it clear from a young age, while Camille and Cara had wanted different paths. Chloe loved the island and volunteered for everything from decorating committees to the island health clinic, but Camille's love of history had convinced her to choose college on the mainland instead. A turn of events had brought her back, but she still remembered the sting of feeling like number two in the family.

Being number two in Maddox May's thoughts the night he broke her heart was the other reason.

Camille had built a wall between the past and the present. It was the only way she could compartmentalize coming back to her home island and running the risk of being choice number two all over again.

"I'm sure Chloe believed she was doing the right thing, but I have a different view," Camille said as gently as she could. Her family hadn't taken much of a twenty-first-century leap, and her mother still considered the internet a suspicious place. The shop, which her parents had taken over when they were younger than she was, had done fine. Her grandparents had turned over management to her father when he was in his midtwenties because they wanted to give him a purpose, a good reason to stay on the island. Camille's parents had chosen the same strategy for Chloe, but her decision to marry and leave the island opened a door nice and wide for Camille. Now Camille wanted to turn it into a regional or even national success. But she didn't want to trample on her parents' feelings in the process.

She smiled at her mom and relaxed the tension in her jaw. "I'm so glad you asked me to come home and take over now that Chloe is moving on."

Camille didn't want to say moving *away* from the island, because she knew her mother's feelings about that subject were somewhere between ecstatic her oldest had found true love and devastation that Chloe's perfect sugarplum-themed bedroom would soon be empty. Growing up, Camille couldn't have imagined their tight family of five ever being apart, but getting away from the island after she graduated had been her life preserver.

Melinda smiled at her daughter. "I knew when we sent you to college you'd come back someday smarter than the rest of us, and if getting our candy to people in places we'll never see is something you think we should do, then of course your father and I support you. We have to let go of some old ideas if we want you to take over."

There were a few qualifying statements and caveats in that less-than-glowing endorsement, but Camille shook it off. Her family would come around when the first waves of success began rolling in. *Change is hard*, she reminded herself, and people who had never left Christmas Island for any serious amount of time probably didn't realize how much the outside world had marched on. Despite her history degree, Camille had found work—ironically—at a candy company in Chicago, where she worked her way up to distribution manager when the company recognized her passion and knowledge regarding candy.

"But you won't change the company name, will you?" her mother asked.

Camille smiled. "Absolutely not. Being associated with Christmas Island is a huge selling point for us. It reminds people of vacations, even if they've never been here. Islands are always a fantasy somehow, and it will go over well in our advertising and the feature articles I'm hoping will run this month in two lifestyle magazines."

"It scares me."

"Trust me," Camille said.

Melinda put a hand over her breast. "I better get in there and box up some fudge before we get so busy we can't turn around. Day visitors will be arriving soon on the first ferry."

Camille nodded and watched her mother enter through the screened door that closed with a satisfying and familiar bang. That same door had been keeping flies out of the candy store all Camille's life, and it was one of the many things about her family's business she didn't want to change. It was on one side of the list she'd made up last spring when she was trying to decide if she should quit her job in Chicago and come home to Christmas Island. Her initial reaction was a decided *no way*. She didn't want to follow in Chloe's footsteps, and she didn't want to be invited just because child number one would no longer be available upon her marriage.

But then she'd started a comparison chart: reasons to go home on one side and reasons not to on the other. The screen door's snap, her love for her family, summer air, the aroma of fudge and the incredible untapped potential of the business made the list of good reasons to board the ferry home. The list of reasons not to were manageable as long as she remembered that wide black line—practically a wall—she'd drawn down the center of the page. She wouldn't fall back into being number two in her family, and she wouldn't let Maddox May's betrayal seven years ago make her feel as if she lacked importance.

She was done with devaluing herself and ready to come home and add value to Island Candy and Fudge in a big way. The happy thought and the sun on her shoulders lifted her spirits as she considered getting a new awning for the shop. Should it be pink and white, or would Christmas colors make a better image for the online and print advertising? Candy colors were true to the product, but red and green might sell the Christmas Island magic even better. Would her family object to a color change if she left the business name the same?

As she pondered, she saw two other people reflected in the shop windows—a tall man and a little boy with a golden retriever.

She recognized them immediately. Maddox May and his son.

"Are you the candy lady?"

Camille had planned to ignore them, thinking if she stayed still enough, maybe they wouldn't even notice her. But it wasn't the child's fault he was the product of a foolish fling that turned into a short-lived marriage to a woman Maddox hardly even knew.

She turned and smiled at the boy. He had dark hair and eyes like his dad. She thought he was tall for his age—six, since he had been born in the spring of her freshman year of college, less than a year after Maddox had kissed another girl and broken Camille's heart. Camille had heard about the boy's birth from her family and promptly tried to forget it.

Looking at his sweet face reminded her that some elements of the past obviously could not stay there. And those elements were the hardest to manage.

"I run the candy shop, so I think that makes me the candy lady," she said. Being nice to kids was a wise business decision for the owner of a candy store. She knelt so she was eye level with the boy. "I'm Camille, and my favorite kind of fudge is maple."

"I'm Ethan. I like chocolate."

She nodded. "I also like chocolate, and I get to smell it all day, which is lucky for me."

"Do you make all the candy?"

Camille laughed, glad the boy was carrying his end of the conversation so she wouldn't have to look at the man standing behind him. "I do make candy, but not all of it. I have help."

"My dad's brought me here lots of times," Ethan said. "I always get a bag of stuff to take home to my mom's."

Camille stood and stepped back. His mom. The woman Maddox had chosen over her with barely a thought. She swallowed and kept a polite smile on her face. "I'm sure your mom likes that."

The boy shook his head. "She doesn't like candy. I eat it all myself."

That wall Camille had constructed to shut out the past was one of her best ideas ever. The fact that the boy she'd thought was her true love had cheated on her was bad enough, but to throw her love away for a woman who didn't even like candy... that was an insult she'd be wise to remember if she ever decided to put a window in that wall.

"Come in and get some treats if it's okay with your dad," she said, the words sounding strange to her. Maddox was definitely a dad—she'd come to grips with that years ago. But it still seemed strange. The past seven years for him had been vastly different from her time since high school.

"I'm not going to my mom's for a long time," Ethan said.

Camille looked at Maddox at last. He nodded slightly to affirm his son's statement. Why wasn't the boy going back to the mainland? Camille tried to avoid any conversation involving Maddox, and most people were cautious about mentioning him around her, because the whole island knew how their high school love affair had ended. But this piece of information sounded like it had a story behind it. No one had told her anything about Maddox's son moving in with his dad permanently.

Did the recent inheritance from Flora Winter have anything to do with the change?

"Can I get candy anyway?" the child asked.

His sweet little voice brought Camille back to the present, and she reached down and touched his shoulder. "Come in and I'll find you something really special, but you have to leave your dog outside." She pointed to a leash hook near the window frame with a bowl of water beneath it.

Inviting Maddox and his son into her shop was either foolish or very wise. It would be her opportunity to prove to herself that the past was the past. She could handle this. Camille took a breath as they walked through the doors, and the notes of chocolate, vanilla and maple in the air bolstered her confidence. She was a candy seller at heart, and clearly the boy could be a valuable off-season and regular customer. Why wasn't he going back to his mother on the mainland anytime soon? She shouldn't care or be interested. Her connection with Maddox had been snapped off like a chunk of peanut brittle the summer she turned eighteen.

MADDOX HAD BEEN inside Island Candy and Fudge hundreds of times in his life. His son loved visiting the store, and the Peterson family was always polite to him despite his breakup with Camille. However, he had avoided the shop all summer. Walking into the store knowing he could come face-to-face with her was too…messy. He told himself he was staying away for her sake.

Maddox remembered so many trips through the screen door that slammed behind him and shut out the island flies. Beautiful Camille and her sisters, always dressed in pink while working in the shop, were fixtures there after school and on the weekends. He understood the obligations of helping in the family business, as he and his brother worked the ferry side by side with their parents. It was life for islanders, and many of his friends knew the daily struggles of keeping a seasonal business afloat.

Of course he and his brother had experienced a major turn of events lately. A gift of millions from their honorary grandmother didn't diminish how hard they'd worked to run their ferry and hotel, and they were planning to work twice as hard with the opportunity provided by such an infusion of cash. Two ferries, another hotel...he and Griffin were only beginning the expansions that would define their futures. Maddox wanted to pass something down to his son that was rich in family history and also success.

"Nothing too messy," he told his son. "You have to help sell ferry tickets in the office while I check on the engines, and you can't get chocolate on the tickets."

"Can't I help with the boat?" Ethan asked.

"Later. Plenty of time."

"But school starts tomorrow," the boy said as he pointed to chocolate-covered pretzels in the glass case.

"First grade?" Camille asked.

Maddox nodded. He figured she'd counted backward to guess his age. Ethan had turned six the previous spring and completed a year of kindergarten on the mainland. But he and his ex-wife had agreed that Ethan would do first grade on the island as a trial run. Maddox hoped it would go well and his son would be his every fall, winter and spring. Summers were harder, with his schedule on the ferry boat, and Ethan usually spent most of the summer with his mother.

Winters had been lonely without him, and Maddox hoped that was going to change. There was no place to grow up like Christmas Island. He wanted Ethan to ice-skate and snowmobile and celebrate Christmas just as he had. Snow-covered island roads, warm fires, the smell of pine... Everything about the island was perfect.

"Mrs. Murray is still teaching first grade," Camille commented, bringing his thoughts back to the scent of chocolate instead of pine and heat instead of crisp winter afternoons.

Maddox laughed. "I know. I thought she was old when we were in first grade, but she probably wasn't even thirty."

They smiled at each other, the shared memory bridging a gap for just a moment. Should he take a chance at breaking the ice with Camille?

"I remember sitting next to you by the window," he said. "You had the desk that creaked every time you turned around to talk to me, so we both got in trouble."

Camille's smile slipped away. *Wrong move.* Camille wasn't ready to reminisce about their childhood, and he couldn't force a friendship with her, no matter how much better he'd feel if they were on friendly terms.

She seemed warm to his son, which didn't really surprise him. Camille was a sweet, kind person whom he'd known better than anyone outside his own family growing up. The familiar wave of guilt over his foolish kiss with an island visitor hit him, but he fought it away. He couldn't spend his life paying for that mistake. He'd lost Camille's love, but the love of his son was worth it. No one could change the past.

What if he and Camille had stayed together? Would they have a child by now? The thought hit him like an unexpected wave. What if the boy at his side was theirs…

"Thank you," he heard his son say to the girl behind the register. She was a teenager, a summer worker he didn't know. Most of the island businesses hired extra help for the season, but Labor Day weekend marked the end of summer, when the island would slowly empty out until it was just the year-round residents, whose names, addresses and pets' names he knew by heart.

"Good luck at school," Camille said. She stood on the other side of the candy counter, smiling at Ethan. "I recommend a seat by the window, especially on sunny days like this one. You can see the lake."

"That's better than my old school, where you could only see the dumpster out the window," Ethan said.

Camille laughed. "Then I'm very glad you're here. The place where I used to work had a view of a highway, so I know what you mean."

Maddox wanted to ask details about Camille's life in Chicago. Had she missed the island? Was she only coming home because her sister was getting married, or was there more to it? Had she ever thought of him as she stared out the window at the highway view?

But instead of asking, Maddox paid for his son's treats and nodded a goodbye to Camille. She made eye contact but only gave him a sliver of a smile. He put a hand on Ethan's shoulder and steered him into the street, where they retrieved Skipper and then walked the sidewalk toward the ferry dock.

The lake breeze blew away the painful memories of a time in his life when he'd made a choice with long-lasting consequences. He'd made a similar choice several years later, when he had to face a failed marriage and a failing ferry boat line and admit he needed help.

His brother's help.

Griffin had been partway through an engineering degree in college when Maddox had to make the incredibly humbling call to his brother that still haunted him. Had he done the right thing by crushing his brother's dream? He'd asked Griffin to come home to pull the family together, rescue the business and confront their father's frail health. It was the only thing he could do.

Family had brought Maddox this far, and the boy at his side was the next generation of the family. There was no room or reason for regret.

"Bulldozer," Ethan said as he pointed toward the docks ahead of him.

Maddox smiled at his son's excitement.

He felt the same way seeing the progress starting on the second ferry boat slip that would allow the expansion of their business to two boats for the following summer, and perhaps more after that.

"They dropped it off Saturday so they'll be ready to start working tomorrow morning," Maddox said.

"But I have to go to school and miss it," Ethan said.

"I'll take pictures. And you can come watch right after school. I promise you they won't get this all done in one day, and there will be plenty of fun stuff for you to see."

This was undoubtedly true. At one time, he and Griffin had planned a slow expansion of their dock in stages as they found the funding for it. It would have taken years. Now, with a cash infusion, they could move quickly—but construction done right would still take time. The northern Michigan winters with their ice would be brutal on hasty construction, and both the May brothers wanted their investment to have a solid foundation.

Maddox walked Ethan to the ticket office, where Dorothy was at work. She'd run the office since he was a little boy. He remembered slipping butterscotch candies from her desk drawer when his parents left him with Dorothy while his dad piloted the ferry and his mother helped with the passengers. Since his mother had retired to Texas to live with her sister, Dorothy had taken her role as stand-in grandmother seriously.

"Candy already?" she asked, pointing to the bag with its signature pink colors. "I hope you have something in there to share with me."

Ethan held open his candy bag and offered the older lady first choice. Maddox smiled at his sweet son, the light of his life and his reason for wanting to be the best father and business owner he could be. He hated to leave him and go to work, but pouring his energy into the family business would be worth the sacrifice.

"Don't eat it all," he told his son as he dropped a kiss on top of his head and headed out to the docks.

CHAPTER THREE

ALTHOUGH THE PETERSON family's business was decorated in bright candy colors, their home several streets back from the waterfront in downtown Christmas Island had gray siding, black shingles and shutters, and a decorative white fence accenting a small flower garden in the front yard. No pink curtains were visible in the living room windows and chocolate chips didn't sprout from the landscaping, even though the girls' bedrooms were still the pastel candy colors from their childhoods. At Christmastime, the house exploded with color and light, but the rest of the year it was a refuge, with only a subtle candy cane wreath on the front door.

The house had a quiet dignity from the outside, but inside, the atmosphere was bursting with excitement. Camille gathered with her sisters around the computer in the nook between the living and dining rooms, and she could barely breathe. It was real. The feature she'd hoped for in *Sweet as Candy* magazine had come to fruition. Camille leaned over and touched the computer screen. A huge photo of Island Candy and Fudge graced the front cover of the online edition, and the editor had promised her print copies were in the mail.

"Flip to the inside pages," Chloe said, her voice rising a notch with excitement as Cara clicked through until she got to the article about their family's business. Camille stood behind the ancient computer chair with one of her mother's colorful handmade afghans hanging over the back. She was too nervous to sit at the computer herself. The publicity was incredible and everything she'd wanted. She'd been home only a few months, and already she was adding her own flavor to the candy business.

"Dinner," her mother called from the kitchen. It was homemade mac and cheese night, one of Camille's favorites, but she couldn't eat until she'd skimmed the article.

"Wow," Chloe said. "I can't believe you

got a spot in the holiday edition. I sent them a letter every year for the past five years."

Camille didn't want to make her sister feel bad by telling her that she'd sent letters, called, emailed and repeated all three strategies until she finally got a tiny bite from the editor. And then she'd written a draft of the article herself and sent high-quality photographs. If the magazine was offered an article that practically wrote itself, why wouldn't they take her up on it?

"I was just lucky," Camille said. "Timing must have been right."

Chloe's excited expression faded. "Maybe this is a bad time for me to get married and leave the island. What if business takes off and you can't—"

Camille was very glad Chloe stopped herself before she finished that statement. Her older sister had done a solid job of helping her parents run the store, but Camille had plans that would go far beyond just getting the job done. And she could handle it. She'd worked in a large candy distribution company for three years before coming home, and volume was something she understood. Despite her intentions to devote herself to the field of history, Camille had lost her enthusiasm for digging around in the past and had gravitated toward something she had an emotional connection to: candy. Working for a high-demand candy company had been good experience, even though it didn't exactly fill her with satisfaction.

The huge company in Chicago may have lacked a personal touch, but it did ship candy to six continents. That was one of the points she was bold enough to make in the article in front of her on the computer. *Under new management from one of the family's daughters, who had relevant experience at Sweet Chicago Candy Company, and is newly home to revitalize Island Candy and Fudge.* Camille shivered when she thought about the pressure she was heaping on herself like a hard shell of candy coating.

"I like the part about you," Cara said quietly as she pointed to the paragraph about Camille coming home to take over. "You're going to do great."

Chloe turned away and went to the dinner table, where Camille and Cara could hear her offering to pour the drinks. Chloe, who was always on hand to be the good and obedient daughter. It was impossible to hate Chloe for her perfection, or even dislike her. She was an openhearted, happy person who had only recently developed a serious case of self-doubt that marred her perfection. Meeting Dr. Dan Williamson when he filled in for the physician who visited the island medical clinic on Wednesdays had changed Chloe's life.

"It'll be okay," Cara said. "Chloe made the choice to leave long before you decided to come home. She doesn't have to compete with you, and your success won't diminish hers." Cara grinned. "Even if you are the middle child and, technically, the second choice for taking over the family empire."

Camille laughed. Cara had been so aware of Camille's role as number two her entire life that Cara had never even asserted herself as number three. She simply went a different route, where her place in the pecking order didn't matter.

"You know you want to look," Cara said. She got up and pointed at the chair. "Do it."

Camille grinned at her sister, sat down

and opened the reports screen of their on-line ordering system. The system was just a few months old and was one of the first things she had implemented. Each customer who purchased a box of fudge or a bag of candy had gone home with a business card emblazoned with the company's website in large letters.

Slowly, the online orders had trickled in. Camille had spreadsheets detailing which products customers were likely to go home and order. The brief questionnaire on the checkout screen also provided valuable information. Was it a reorder of the same thing they had purchased on the island, a different flavor of the same kind of product, a gift for a friend?

Targeted research and marketing. Camille had three months of information, and she had tweaked and redesigned the webpage each week as she evaluated what was selling. The article in the national magazine highlighted her best online sellers.

She took a deep breath and glanced at her younger sister for courage, and then she clicked on the orders screen.

"Oh, my goodness," she said. Her mouth

opened in shock. There were dozens of orders already.

"Hit Refresh," Cara said.

The number jumped again when the new screen loaded.

Camille's heart raced, and she exchanged an incredulous smile with Cara.

"Dinner's getting cold," her mother called from the kitchen. "Camille, I know it's your favorite, and I put on extra crumb topping this time."

Camille walked into the kitchen and paused in the doorway. "The article is working. We've gotten over a hundred orders just today, and they're rolling in fast."

Her mother held the serving spoon in the air over the casserole dish she'd been using all Camille's life. How many family meals had been baked to perfection in that very dish? Some things were perfect just as they were, but would her family understand why she wanted to breathe new life into Island Candy and Fudge?

Camille thought her mother looked almost frightened, which frustrated her. She'd explained her plans to scale the production up to handle the new business. The family business could handle this. Hadn't her mother been listening all the times Camille had explained to her what she did in her previous job and how she was going to grow their candy business? Did the family understand that when Camille said *growth* she meant boxes and crates of candy leaving the island in massive shipments? What if she hadn't prepared them enough?

"How will we make all that candy?" her father asked.

"I showed you my plan," Camille said. "And I know you think it's pretty ambitious and maybe a little scary, but we can do this." She hoped she conveyed absolute competence, but inside she felt as if she had two racetracks with cars going in opposite directions. There was no going back, no taking second place in her own life or in her family. She was moving forward and taking Island Candy and Fudge along for the ride.

Chloe gave her a shaky smile. "Our little candy store will never be the same."

Camille didn't answer, not wanting to wade into a family argument. Of course the island candy business was wonderful, but it didn't have to stay the same.

"We should eat before dinner gets cold," her mother said.

Camille sat at her usual place at the table and forked into the mac and cheese casserole. Cara shot her an encouraging smile. It might take a while, but her parents and Chloe would come around, and Camille planned to work hard to earn their approval. Hard work was the only thing that led to success, and things that seemed to come too easily were destined to fail. She'd learned that the hard way.

CARRYING A FILING cabinet on one shoulder, Maddox kept his free hand on the railing as he ascended the stairs at the Winter Palace. The Victorian-style mansion was the grandest home on Christmas Island and had been in Flora Winter's family her entire life. Now that she was in her mid-eighties, she'd decided that Griffin and Maddox May would be the next owners of the beautiful island home overlooking the lake from a bluff.

"I thought you said Rebecca didn't have much stuff," he grumbled to his brother.

"She doesn't," Griffin said. "That's my filing cabinet. Thanks for hauling it up to the third floor for me."

"You owe me," Maddox said.

"I'll pay your babysitter this evening," Griffin said. "Dorothy tonight?"

Maddox nodded. "She's the best. She's probably letting Ethan eat ice cream for dinner and Skipper sit on the couch."

Griffin laughed. "I hope so."

In addition to helping Rebecca arrange her living and working space on the middle floor of the mansion, Maddox's brother was also moving in. He would take the third floor, where he'd have a perfect view of lake conditions—ideal for a person who owned a ferry line. Hearing an engagement announcement from his brother and Rebecca in the near future wouldn't surprise Maddox at all. Maddox wasn't jealous of his brother for being the one to move into the mansion. He could easily find room for himself and his son if he wanted to, but the family home, where he'd grown up, had become his, and he wanted his son to grow up in the modest but cozy home. He and Griffin had agreed to use some of their inheritance to add a deck, fenced-in backyard and jungle gym to the single-story home, and Maddox expected to be perfectly happy there with his son by his side, reliving some of the memories from his own childhood and making plenty of their own.

Maddox cleared the landing and entered the living area on the top floor. Flora Winter had used the space for herself when she was younger, and it had flowery curtains and rugs. Even though the thick rugs were expensive and in good condition, it was funny thinking about his brother's big bare feet resting on bunches of pink flowers.

"I know," Griffin said without waiting for Maddox to comment. "I may redecorate this winter when things slow down."

"It may grow on you and you'll become a lace-curtains kind of guy," Maddox said. He looked out the window at the lake. It was early September and the trees were still green. It wouldn't be long before the fall color came. "This is way nicer than your old apartment. I pity the next per-

son who moves in and finds out the floors
creak and the windows don't do much to
keep out the winter wind."

"I told her about that."

"Her?"

"Camille Peterson," Griffin said. "She's
there right now measuring for curtains and
whatever else she needs. I think she's anxious to get out of her parents' house and get
settled before the Halloween and Christmas
candy rush."

"You haven't even totally moved out,"
Maddox said. He shouldn't care what Camille's plans were, and it shouldn't feel
personal picturing her in the same space
where he and his brother had kicked back
and watched television on winter nights.
Everyone had a right to move onward and
upward. Camille was back, and she wanted
to move out of her childhood home. He
was making his childhood home his own
for himself and his son. It was as simple
as that.

"I just have a few things left there," Griffin said. "I told her I'd be back for them
later this evening."

Maddox dropped the lace curtain over

the window. It was almost too dark to see the lake anyway. The days were getting noticeably shorter, which was all the more reason to finish up the moving so he and his brother could get down to business on their ferry dock before winter hit.

"Griffin," a voice called up the stairs. "I need a little help when you have a minute."

Maddox smiled at his brother. "You go help Rebecca. I'll pick up the rest of your stuff from your old place so we can get this knocked out and get back to work."

"Thanks," Griffin said, already breezing past Maddox and heading for the stairs. "There's a box on the kitchen table and one set of boots by the door. And my bike is on the landing. If you don't mind risking an awkward—"

"Box, boots, bike," Maddox interrupted as he followed his older brother down the stairs. He heard Rebecca explaining that the cellar door was stuck open and she was afraid of bats entering in the dark. Maddox chuckled. The Winter Palace, despite its grandeur, was an old mansion on an island. It had probably hosted a few bats over the years. Rebecca had lived there for three months as Flora's summer companion, but fall and winter on the island were going to be a fun experience for her. Christmas Island took its name seriously, with holiday celebrations that stretched on for weeks.

Maddox got in the truck the brothers shared and drove downtown. With their inheritance, they could afford to get another vehicle, but that would take time out of their tight schedule. Most of the stores were dark; day visitors left the island early on fall evenings—another sign that the building season was getting short. The island came alive again between Thanksgiving and Christmas, and then it would settle into a peaceful slumber until the next summer season. Maddox loved the change of seasons, but summer was the most important one to his business. They had to be ready for the first rush when the ice cleared, schools emptied and families were ready for summer holidays.

In contrast to the dark windows downtown, the lights in his brother's former apartment over a store were on. Maddox sighed. He doubted Camille wanted to see him in her new place. Moving out of her parents' home was almost certainly part of her plan to move her family's business and herself into the next phase of life. Did she ever take a moment to look backward?

Maddox parked and entered through the street door that led to interior stairs. He paused on the landing at the top of the steps. He had a key, but this was Camille's apartment now. Sort of. He knocked.

"Griffin?" Without waiting for an answer, she opened the door, a tape measure in one hand. When she saw him, her face clearly showed her disappointment. She looked like a woman who'd ordered dessert and gotten a side of broccoli instead.

"Sorry," he said.

"For what?"

Maddox considered his answer. He was sorry for a lot of things, but apologies were so overdue and inadequate that there was no use. Moving forward was the only thing that made any sense, even though the past was a grand piano hanging from a tenuous wire over their heads.

"Barging in on you in your new place," he said.

"It's not mine officially until tomorrow,

but your brother let me in tonight so I could think about what I want to bring and how I want to arrange it. I may have to go shopping tomorrow in Lakeside for the usual stuff you need in a new place."

"Did you have a nice place in Chicago?" he asked. He knew she'd lived there since college, and he'd tried to imagine her walking the city streets, riding public transportation with strangers. Had she missed the island where everyone knew her name?

"It was tiny. This place feels huge and has a much better view."

Maddox nodded. "I'm sure it will look a lot nicer than it ever did when Griffin lived here. He was working all the time, so he hardly spent time here."

Camille waited without speaking, as if hoping her silence would encourage him to leave. At one time in their lives, they could talk for hours, never running out of things to say. They'd talked about school, their families, their plans for the future. Maddox longed to talk about those things now. He had friends, of course, and his brother. But the bond he'd shared with Camille was something he'd never found in anyone else.

He swallowed and forced himself to be practical and keep moving forward even though his heart wanted to retrace the footprints he and Camille had left on the island trails. "I'll just grab the three *B*s and get out of here."

"The three *B*s?" Camille asked.

"Griffin asked me to pick up a box, boots and his bike. He's helping Rebecca with something at the house they'll basically be sharing, so I volunteered to finish clearing out here."

"That's nice," Camille said. "Cara was going to come along and help me measure, but Chloe wanted her help deciding on exactly what kind of white roses to order for the bridesmaids' bouquets."

"There are different kinds of white roses?"

Camille smiled for the first time. "Apparently."

"Poor Cara," Maddox said, and he felt his heart lift when Camille laughed. For a long time, he'd been certain he would never share a joke with Camille or hear her sweet laugh again. Was it possible they could be friends now that they were both home?

"I could help you measure," Maddox offered, hoping to find a way to build on the tentative bridge between them.

Camille tucked the tape measure in her jacket pocket. "I was all done," she said. She took one more look around the apartment. "I'm heading home."

Disappointment crowded out the brief optimism Maddox had felt.

"But I can carry one of the three *B*s down while I'm going," she said.

Maddox smiled. "Do you want the box, the boots or the bike?"

"I think the box is the safest choice," she said.

Maddox had taken the safe route with Camille all summer. He'd given her space, tried to be friendly without being too familiar. It was exhausting, always dancing around the chasm between them. What if they were meeting for the first time? Would they have the same chemistry that had drawn them together nearly a decade ago? Was there a time limit on first or second chances?

Camille picked up the box from the kitchen table. "It's nice of your brother to leave me the table and chairs," she said.

Maddox nodded. "The Winter Palace has more furniture than he needs."

He didn't need to say that Griffin could afford to buy a thousand kitchen tables and chairs if he wanted to. The money was giving them the chance to build their family business, but otherwise it wasn't going to change them. Camille seemed to be building her own family's business by herself without an influx of cash. She had determination and intelligence to spare.

"I hope he'll be happy there," Camille said.

Maddox reached over and tucked the flaps closed on the box in Camille's arms. It was the closest he had been to her all summer, and the temptation to touch her, even kiss her, was so strong he stepped back abruptly and almost lost his balance when he backed into a chair.

"Are your sea legs failing you?" Camille asked with a hint of a smile.

Maddox swallowed. "Just off balance for a minute."

He didn't need to explain why. The flush that came to her cheeks right before she spun and headed for the door told him she understood what had put him off-kilter. Would they have a chance to be alone or even talk anytime soon? There were always other people around. His family. Her family. Their friends. Island workers and residents. Something made him want to grasp the moment.

"Are we ever going to talk about it?" he asked right before she got to the door.

She stopped but didn't turn. If he could only see her eyes, her expression…

"Is there anything new to say?" she asked, her voice a low neutral that offered no encouragement.

"A lot has changed."

She shook her head. "You can't change the past."

With those words, she walked down the steps. Maddox flipped on the light switch to illuminate her way. He couldn't change the past. All he could do was build a future for his son and himself.

CHAPTER FOUR

A WEEK LATER, Camille drove her Ford Escape onto the ferry. With one cautious glance, she'd noted Griffin in the wheelhouse. Most island visitors might have difficulty telling the brothers apart. They were both tall, broad shouldered and dark haired, with eyes that matched the blue lake.

Not that Camille was thinking about his eyes. Her plan for the day was to drive to the truck rental outside Lakeside and exchange her Escape for a refrigerated box truck. It was one of the boldest things she had ever done. Right up there with breaking up with her high school sweetheart, leaving Christmas Island, striding confidently onto a college campus, working for a Chicago candy company and then being brave enough to circle back to where she started.

Well, not exactly where she started. The

Island Candy and Fudge Company had never rented a vehicle, and certainly not a massive truck. She was going places and taking the family business with her. The magazine article had blown up their website, so they'd had to crank up their production and hire more people. The candy had to ship somehow, and the tiny Christmas Island post office was no match for the volume she had in mind.

Her distribution plan involving her newly rented mainland building was her best hope for success.

"Taking a trip?" Griffin asked as he appeared at her driver's window.

She knew he would tell his brother he'd seen her on the ferry, and she considered giving him a whopper of a story. Though maybe the truth was its own far-fetched tale. Camille plastered a bold smile on her face. "I certainly am. I'm going to rent a delivery truck, because my plan to sell online and ship candy anywhere in the country is going well."

Griffin smiled. "It must be. How big a truck are you getting?"

"Don't worry. It'll fit on your ferry,"

she said. Camille had selected the truck from the rental company's website. It was somewhere between family van and moving truck, but she didn't want to admit she had no way to describe it in cubic feet or whatever he was asking. "And I know I have to pay extra."

"Only if it has more than two axles," Griffin said. He waited, and Camille tried to remember the picture of the truck from the website. Were there more than two rows of tires? Instead of admitting she wasn't sure, she returned Griffin's curious glance.

"How many tons of cargo will this ferry hold?"

"Way more than that truck will."

"Good," she said. "Because I think that's how much Halloween candy we've already sold, and I can't even imagine what Christmas is going to be like."

"I'll tell my brother to keep an eye out for you. I'm taking the morning run, and then he's in the pilothouse the rest of the day." Griffin smiled, tapped the side of her car and moved back across the ferry toward the pilothouse. Two minutes later, the horn sounded, and the Christmas Island ferry chugged away from the dock toward the mainland in the distance. Camille had made the trip many times in her life, often with a vehicle for shopping trips that weren't within walking distance of the mainland ferry dock.

Feeling restless, she got out and paced the deck until the ferry approached the shore. Knowing Maddox would be waiting for her when she returned driving a massive rental truck added a layer of worry to her already-taut nerves. Was she out of her mind, increasing candy production exponentially and getting behind the wheel of the candy express?

Camille let out a breath as she got back behind the wheel and got ready to disengage the parking brake and roll off the ferry. She could do this.

Two hours later, she wasn't so sure. She had instructions for operating the lift gate on the back that could accommodate an astonishing three thousand pounds of candy at a time. The air-conditioning and automatic transmission worked the same as her car. However, she felt like a giant trying to crawl into a dollhouse as she lumbered through the city streets toward the dock in the massive vehicle. The thought of driving it onto the ferry made her stomach crawl up her throat.

She steered into the marked approach lanes for the ferry, where three other vehicles and several tourists on foot waited. Would there be room? She shivered and then reached over and turned off the air-conditioning. She rolled down both windows just in case she needed to hear instructions from the dockhands. One of the older men who worked in the candy kitchen part-time had offered to pick up the truck for her. He had driven trucks in the military and said he'd be honored to complete the mission, but Camille had insisted on going herself.

The tablespoon of doubt in her mind had burgeoned to a two-pound slice of apprehension.

A dockhand waved her forward, and she gingerly inched toward the ramp. She leaned out the window to ask if there was enough room for her, but the dockhand looked annoyed and waved her toward him, his hand motions quick. Maybe she should wait for the next ferry. It was a beautiful day. She was in no hurry. If she was the first person in line, she couldn't possibly hit any other cars as she squeezed the massive truck onto the ferry that suddenly seemed small.

"Problem?"

Camille recognized the voice at the passenger window of her truck. No way was she letting Maddox May know that her pulse was racing and cold fear ran over her even with the air-conditioning off and the warm September air wafting through the windows.

Maddox stood on the running board so he was eye level right outside the window. Only the width of the seat separated them, and he was close enough for her to remember how much she'd once loved his deep blue eyes.

"I'm just not sure there's enough room for this truck on your boat," she said, pulling her thoughts in a safer direction.

"There's plenty of room."

"I'm waiting for instructions from the dockhand."

A hint of smile tipped the edges of Maddox's mouth. "I think he's going to wear out his arms waving you on board."

"I was just—"

"It'll be fine," he said. "I'll ride right here and let you know if you're going to hit anything."

Marvelous, Camille thought. In her biggest challenge of the day, the person who had taken her middle-child uncertainty and tied the heavy weight of his infidelity to it was going to be a ride-along. This could not get much worse.

Camille wanted to roll up the window as a shield from Maddox, but what if she really needed to hear a warning? She couldn't risk running someone over or bashing into the ferry or another vehicle. She was going to have to steel herself for the tight squeeze onto the boat.

Camille put the truck in gear and rolled forward, trying to think about how good she was going to get at this task because the Island Candy and Fudge Company would be shipping tons of treats. She held her breath as her front wheels caught the edge of the ramp and bounced.

"You're doing fine. Steady ahead," Maddox said.

She knew she was doing fine. The dockhand wasn't looking panicked. He looked bored, as if he was wondering when the lady in the giant truck with a refrigerator unit hanging over the cab was going to finally put that beast in the only remaining vehicle spot.

Camille eased the rear wheels onto the ferry and took a moment to celebrate her accomplishment. The truck was off dry land, and nothing bad had happened. Its weight hadn't sunk the ferry, and she hadn't even raised an eyebrow among the passengers waiting. She could do this. She *was* doing it.

"Go ahead and park it here so we balance the weight," Maddox said. "Don't forget the parking brake."

"I know," Camille said. "It's not my first time driving a vehicle onto the ferry."

At his small smile, she could guess what he was thinking. *It's not every day your ex–high school sweetheart drives a massive truck onto your ferry.*

"Is this going to be a daily occurrence

now that you're expanding the candy business?"

She considered telling him about her plan to produce candy in a building she'd rented on the mainland. The building had been empty for years, and she'd gotten it for just pennies a square foot using her personal savings until the idea proved itself. Producing candy there for shipping would mean she'd cut out the ferry passage. For the moment, she was using her new facility as a staging area for shipping candy produced on the island, but as soon as she got through the Christmas rush, she planned to produce and package there. But there was no reason to share her plans with Maddox. Once she would've shared her dreams with him, but a lot of time had passed since then.

"Maybe," she said. "But I only have two axles on this truck, so you can't charge me extra."

"I wasn't worried about the charge. I just thought I might have to adjust the ferry schedule and add more time at the dock if you're going to drive on at snail speed."

Camille opened her mouth to protest that she'd actually done just fine, thank you very much, but Maddox had hopped down and was striding toward the steps to the pilothouse. She closed her mouth. She didn't need his approval or anyone else's.

MADDOX STOOD IN the pilothouse and watched the huge truck lumber off his ferry. Either Camille was feeling more confident driving it, or she was anxious to get away from him. Everyone on the dock looked her way as the truck clanked over the ramp, including the man who was running the excavator working on the new portion of dock. The arm of the excavator swung in a big arc, and Camille swerved away from it even though it looked to Maddox like she didn't need to. The excavator driver was a professional, and there was no doubt he saw her yellow rental truck.

When Camille swerved, she ran into a luggage cart parked on the dock waiting for hotel guests. The truck lurched to a stop, and Maddox watched Camille slide out of the driver's seat. Even from a distance, she looked shaken as she dashed around the truck. Did she think she had run over something valuable or, worse yet, a person? She put a hand over her heart when she saw that the only casualty was an old luggage cart.

Dorothy came out of the office and put an arm around Camille as she pointed to the mangled cart. It was nice of the older lady, but Maddox was the ferry captain and co-owner of the ferry line. It was his responsibility to address any incidents or damage done on his watch.

He swung down the steps, his feet hardly touching them, and loped across the boat's deck. Though the truck had barely cleared the boat, it had all its wheels on solid ground. This was a property issue, not a maritime one. He could have called his brother and had him review the damage with Camille, but he wasn't going to weasel out of his job.

"No one hurt?" he asked as he approached, even though he'd seen the whole thing and already knew the answer.

"I may have permanent heart damage," Camille said.

Somehow she looked even more flustered than she had a moment ago. The permanent damage to her heart was something

Maddox already knew about, and he'd caused it.

"Nothing that can't be fixed," he said, his voice low.

Camille's expression pinched, but she stopped rubbing the place above her heart. Maybe she'd decided she would survive this encounter. After all, it was just an old cart. And she'd survived worse.

"The machine swung around and I thought we were going to collide," she said.

"I saw," Maddox said. He didn't add that there'd been no possibility of an imminent collision and she'd overreacted. Some things were a lot clearer from a distance and a different perspective. Maddox dropped to his haunches and inspected her truck tire. The cart had splintered and broken in half. No loss. It was ancient and one of the many things he and Griffin had on the replace list.

"Is it bad?" Camille asked.

Maddox glanced up and noticed that Dorothy still had an arm around Camille. Dorothy had lived on the island for decades, and nothing got past her. He was sure she knew how the two high school sweethearts had ended things seven years ago, and he was equally sure there was a chance Dorothy was on Camille's side. Most people had been.

"I don't think it even scratched the paint," he said. "Tire looks fine. I think your truck was the definite victor in the battle with my luggage cart."

"I'll pay for the damage," Camille said.

Maddox shook his head. "Don't. It's not worth worrying about, and we were going to replace it before next year anyway."

"I insist," Camille said. "I'm not going to destroy anything without taking responsibility."

Would he and Camille ever reach a point where everything they said didn't have a double meaning? Yes, he'd destroyed their relationship when he'd kissed Jennifer. And he'd taken refuge in a relationship with her after Camille had broken up with him. It had been a miserable time in his life, with his father's illness and the struggling ferry business, and Jennifer had offered sympathy. He'd also stepped up and taken responsibility when Jennifer became pregnant.

Did he regret the weakness that had led

to that kiss and the breakup? Yes, but he didn't regret the relationship that had given him his son.

"Fine. The total value of that cart is fifteen dollars," he said.

Camille scoffed. "I don't believe that."

"It's true," Dorothy said. "I searched for some used ones on eBay a while back because we wanted to buy one or two extras, and that's what they were going for."

"I'm serious about replacing it anyway," Maddox said. He pointed to the major construction project underway on the shoreline, where the excavator was now moving giant rocks. "We're replacing a lot of older equipment, and that one's heading for the dumpster just a little sooner than the rest."

Camille picked up the splintered board that had comprised the bottom of the luggage cart and examined it, and Dorothy patted her shoulder and then walked back to the ticket office.

"I'm glad this was all I hit." Her voice was low, dejected, and Maddox wanted to reach out and hug her. He wished he could tell her it was no big deal. She needed to not beat herself up over a minor accident.

But he knew she wouldn't see it that way. He knew how much she used to doubt herself and second-guess her choices. Living with perfect Chloe on one side of the family order and carefree Cara on the other had landed Camille squarely in the middle. He'd known how it was hard for her to trust herself and her decisions. He'd known that, and he'd done the one thing that he doubted Camille would ever forgive him for.

The broken luggage cart was forgivable.

"If you want, you can ask Rebecca to put a value on that old thing. You trust her," he said. "We do, too, which is why she's our financial guru now. If she thinks you owe the May Ferry Line a million bucks in damages, I think we can all agree she's right."

Camille's clouded expression eased a little. She and Rebecca had been college roommates, after all. That was how Rebecca had learned of Christmas Island in the first place. Camille would trust her judgment.

"But for now, do you think you can get your truck out of the way? I've got a ferry boat that's already way behind schedule."

"Sorry," Camille said, not looking at him.

"Don't be," Maddox said.

Two cars were waiting in the street because the ferry lanes were still blocked by the big truck. Bicycles dodged around them, and a golf cart blew its horn.

"I'll get this out of here," Camille said. "But I'm asking Rebecca about the damage."

Maddox nodded. "Whatever makes you feel better, but I think you're making too big a deal out of it."

Camille's cheeks pinked, and her mouth pressed into a flat line. Maddox realized he'd said the wrong thing when he remembered that evening before graduation, when he'd confessed to Camille. The night sounds of crickets and waves had been all around them, but there had been dead silence when he'd tried to minimize his actions by telling Camille she was making too big a deal out of his onetime indiscretion.

She stalked to the driver's door, hauled herself up into the seat and started forward past the tourists and the waiting cars. Maddox watched her turn down a side street that would lead to an alley behind the Island Candy and Fudge shop. If he was lucky, his brother would be running the ferry when Camille loaded the truck for the trip to the mainland. He was sure she wouldn't want to see him anytime soon.

CHAPTER FIVE

THE CHRISTMAS ISLAND Craft Show was always the first weekend in October. Camille had a heart full of happy memories from attending every year with her mother and sisters. It was nonnegotiable, the event they never skipped, even during college. Camille would drive straight to Lakeside after her last Friday class to catch the ferry to the island for the weekend.

Most years, she had avoided running into Maddox by keeping her head down. Now, though, Camille knew there was no point in trying to pretend there was a line down the center of the island with one of them on either side. She'd have to see him around.

If there was a line, Maddox seemed comfortable crossing it and being friendly. Was it because he no longer had feelings for her and was able to treat her just like anyone else on the island? Was he simply being friendly to her, just as he would to Violet or Rebecca or her sisters?

"I'm on the hunt for a new Christmas wreath," her mother said as the four Peterson women left their front door and walked toward the church along the waterfront. Situated just outside downtown, the church was a traditional white-shingled structure with a bell tower and a small parking lot. Camille had done her senior project in high school on the history of the church. She'd raised funds for the large black-and-white pictures that hung in the entryway, documenting the church's history.

The church served locals and tourists, and it reaped almost half of its yearly budget from the craft festival. Vendor tables spread beyond the parking lot, through the empty grass lot next door and down the sidewalks. Every year the craft show had grown until it attracted more people from off the island than island residents. Some of the profits were used to fund community celebrations like the Thanksgiving party at the Great Island Hotel, a lavish and beloved local event.

"A new wreath for the house?" Camille asked her mother.

Melinda nodded. "Front door. I debated throwing out the old one when I put it away after Christmas last year, but it's so hard to toss out all the happy memories that went with it. Do you know how many family Christmas card pictures we took in front of the house with that wreath in the background?"

"So did you toss it?" Cara asked.

Their mother looked almost guilty, and she lowered her voice. "I did."

Chloe gasped. "Maybe I would have taken it for my new house."

Camille sighed. "You can get a new one, too. You're starting over, and you don't have to haul your entire history with you."

Camille noticed that Cara cut her a questioning look.

"The past is the past," Camille affirmed, even though she doubted her mother and older sister were listening. They were already admiring the first craft booth they'd encountered, where an artisan had taken old-fashioned wooden sleds and decorated them with painted winter scenes, greenery and ribbons.

"Hey, candy girls."

Camille turned at the friendly and familiar voice. "I'd be annoyed with most people for calling us that." She smiled at Rebecca, her former college roommate and new Island neighbor. "I never should have told you about my childhood nickname."

Rebecca looped an arm through Camille's. "It could be worse. If your parents didn't own a candy shop and instead were plumbers or morticians, imagine the nicknames for their three beautiful daughters."

Camille laughed. "I'm not even going to imagine. You're right. I should start a side business called the Candy Girls."

Rebecca stopped walking, and her expression turned serious. "That's a great idea. You could do cross-over promotion and widen your market. For example, you could focus on high-end mail order chocolates instead of vacation-memory fudge."

"I think I have enough on my candy dish right now," Camille said. "I can't believe I rented a giant truck for last weekend's candy delivery. You should have seen me driving that thing." She didn't want to think about Maddox on the running board talking to her through the open window. He had no right to be a ride-along on her new path.

"I'm impressed. You're a woman who can do it all," Rebecca said.

"I'd like to think I'm moving the family business way forward, but this island has a way of sucking you back into your past until you're up to your knees in it."

Rebecca smiled and shrugged. "Being up to your knees in people who love you doesn't sound so bad."

Camille put an arm around her friend. Rebecca had grown up in the foster care system and never had a home or family to call her own. Coming to Christmas Island at the beginning of the summer and falling in love with the people—and one of them in particular—had changed her life. She glowed with the happiness of love and belonging, and Camille felt a stab of guilt that she took family and belonging lightly.

She didn't take love lightly. In fact, she knew a lot about its power, both good and destructive.

"I'll confess that sometimes I wonder if I should leave everything as it is," Camille said. "Keep making candy and selling it to tourists like we always have."

"How does your family feel about it?"

Camille sighed. "My parents and Chloe are being polite, but I think they wonder why I'm trying so hard when I could just continue on as we always have."

"So why don't you?"

Camille watched her mother and Chloe admiring a table of hand-knitted baby blankets. How long would it be before Chloe and her new husband had kids? Would Chloe push to move back to the island then so her children could have the same childhood she'd had? If she did, would she want to get back into the family business? And where would that leave Camille? She was not going back to being number two in the family.

"I don't want to be number two," she said aloud.

"No one does," Rebecca said, walking next to her as they moved slowly down the line of craft booths. "And don't be ridiculous. You're an adult, and you're not just a middle child anymore. Anyone who knows you is darn sure you're blazing your own glorious trail of chocolate."

Camille pictured herself walking along an endless path of chocolate and sweets. "I like the sound of that."

"Just take me with you, please," Rebecca said. "I don't want you going all alone."

"No one is lonely on this island."

"Certainly not today. Is everyone on the island here?"

"Everyone plus a whole lot of people from the mainland who come to do their Christmas shopping. Years ago, they used to have the festival closer to Christmas, but the weather was too unpredictable for running the ferries that late in the fall."

Someone had a fire going, and the air smelled of wood smoke, leaves, coffee and the homemade doughnuts Camille knew they were frying in the church kitchen.

Cara caught her eye as she held up a garden spinner with glittering horses catching the October sun. "What do you think? I could hang it above the entrance at the horse barn to try to discourage the barn swallows from building in the overhang and pooping on me."

"What if they like it and they bring their whole family to build there?" Rebecca asked.

Cara laughed. "Then I'll just have to wear a bigger hat."

Just then Maddox appeared, holding Ethan's hand as they walked toward Camille, Rebecca and Cara. Ethan tugged his dad to a stop at a booth with hand-carved wooden toys. Maddox leaned down and inspected a game with balls and slots. The man running the booth showed Ethan how to play the game, and Maddox straightened up and watched. It reminded Camille of all the times she'd come to the craft festival with her family as a child. Each year, she'd found a treasure to take home. One time it was a wreath for her bedroom that she thought looked very sophisticated. Another year she'd fallen in love with a cut-glass cake plate from one of the antique dealers. Camille and her sisters had saved their money each year for their favorite shopping event.

Would Ethan take home a treasure and

would his dad bring him back every year? Growing up on the island had been magical and safe, with the scents of pines, candy and wood fires flavoring all her memories. She'd been darn glad to leave all that behind when Maddox had trashed her heart. She'd been lucky to have a college acceptance letter on her pink dresser and a good reason to leave with her chin in the air.

Now that she was back, every day was a museum of her childhood mixed with dreams for her future. The wall between the past and future was tough to maintain at events like the Christmas Island Craft Show.

"Fresh doughnuts, just like always," Chloe said, holding a box out to Camille. "They're still warm."

Camille selected one with chocolate icing and sprinkles after she made sure there were at least two of each kind so Rebecca would get her choice. There were no doughnuts anywhere like the fresh ones eaten outdoors at the island festival. Her teeth sank into the perfect texture just as she noticed a woman she hadn't seen in years scoop Ethan May up in her arms.

"Griffin's mom is here for the weekend," Rebecca said, nodding toward the older woman. "She says she never misses it, and she wanted to see what improvements her boys were making with their unexpected windfall."

Camille remembered Jeanette May perfectly. Griffin and Maddox's mother had always seemed overwhelmed. She was sweet but rattled in every one of Camille's memories, as if helping run the ferry line and raise two boys was always too much for her. Even during high school, she'd always seemed as if there was something she needed to rush off to handle.

Looking back on it, Camille knew that Maddox and Griffin's dad had quietly battled cancer for years, not telling his sons until it was too late for him and nearly too late to save the family business. What had compelled Jeanette May to keep the secret? Was she afraid of hurting her husband by violating his confidence, or was she afraid her sons couldn't handle it?

Camille had always wondered if Maddox and Griffin had known, even if they'd never said anything. Had she been as supportive of him during their senior year as he'd needed…or was that why he'd felt the need to kiss another girl?

"She's a nice lady, and I think she's loving life in Texas, where it's always warm and she doesn't have to work as a dockhand on a ferry boat when too many employees call off."

Camille laughed. "A well-deserved retirement." She watched Jeanette May kiss her grandson's cheek and then put him down. She took his hand and led him over to the church entrance where the doughnut stand was set up. Camille wondered if Ethan came each year. She hadn't seen him before, but she'd been careful to keep her eyes on the vendors and not sweep her glance around, looking for trouble.

This year was different, because her new plan was to embrace island life, and she was no longer trying to hide from Maddox.

"I bet he'll want the chocolate sprinkles," Camille said. "Ethan has a sweet tooth and a habit of coming to my shop."

"With his dad?" Rebecca asked.

Camille shrugged. "I believe so."

"He's cute," Rebecca said. "Griffin told him to call me Aunt Rebecca."

Camille raised an eyebrow. "That almost sounds like a proposal."

Rebecca laughed. "Hardly. You know the May brothers use the term *aunt* liberally. Aunt Flora is an obvious example. And Griffin and I have only been together a few months."

"You're living in the same house."

"A mansion. We have separate floors."

Camille laughed. "I doubt walls will keep you two apart."

As she spoke, she noticed Maddox May walking toward her. Her walls were solid, but years of studying history had shown her it took effort to keep them that way.

WITH ONE SWIFT GLANCE, Maddox decided his son would be perfectly happy eating sugary fried dough with his grandmother. He wanted a chance to slip back to the booth where his son had seen the wooden toy so he could buy it for him for Christmas. But he needed an accomplice or he wouldn't get past his son's sharp powers of observation.

Rebecca and Camille stood in the middle of the walkway, and it was too good an opportunity to pass up. Rebecca had already spent time with Ethan, who affectionately called her Aunt Rebecca. Maddox knew she'd help him out. And Camille? Was it taking a stupid chance of rubbing salt in an old wound if he asked for her help shopping for his son?

There was just one way to find out, and he wanted to put his son's happiness at the front of the line. Ethan was going to be part of island life, and there was no reason to shy away from anything.

"Hey," he said as he walked up to them.

"You're not going to steal all our doughnuts, are you?" Rebecca asked.

"Just one," he said. "And I'd be happy to eat whichever one you two don't want."

"What if we want them all?" Camille asked.

"Then I back slowly away," he said, smiling. "But I could actually use some help if you have a minute."

"Sure," Rebecca agreed. Camille didn't say anything, but she didn't shut him down, either.

Maddox pulled some cash from his pocket.

"There's a green-and-blue toy at the front of that table over there."

"The one with the balls and slots," Camille said. "I saw you and Ethan looking at it."

She'd noticed? He shouldn't be flattered. Camille was a smart and observant person. She was also a nice person, so if she agreed to what he was about to ask her, he shouldn't read into it.

He held out the cash. "Will you buy the toy and help me hide it until closer to Christmas?"

Camille's smile faltered, and she hesitated just long enough to make Maddox think she was about to refuse him. Who could blame her? Playing Santa for her ex-boyfriend's child was asking a lot.

"We'd have to be quick while Ethan is with your mother," Camille said.

"Sorry to intrude on your day and pressure you," Maddox said.

"It's okay. The craft festival is the same as always. Same vendors in the same places," Camille said. "It's like time stops the first weekend in October every year."

There were moments in his life Maddox wished could go on forever. Standing in the sunlit fall day with Camille while the scents and sounds of his beloved island were all around him was one of those moments. He wished he could freeze his son at the sweet age of six, when he loved simple things and approached life as if it were magical.

But he couldn't stop time or hide from it. Christmas was coming, his son was growing up fast and if Maddox could control time...well, he wouldn't change everything about his past mistakes, because his errors had given him Ethan.

"I could hide it at the Winter Palace," Rebecca said, bringing his thoughts back to the current issue. "That place is huge, and I haven't even discovered all the hiding places myself yet."

"Thanks," Maddox said. "My house is small, and I'm afraid I can't fool Ethan for long."

"I'll run over and get it before someone else buys it," Rebecca said, taking the cash he still held out.

Rebecca left him standing alone with Camille. They weren't really alone in the crowd of hundreds of people shopping, eating and talking. But they were bound together until Rebecca returned with his son's gift. If Rebecca hadn't jumped in with her offer, would Camille have purchased the gift and hidden it at her apartment until he needed it?

"It's nice that your son gets to come to this festival and all the other fun stuff involved in growing up on this island," Camille said.

"That's what I thought," Maddox said. "That's why I fought for this chance."

"Chance?"

"His mother is getting remarried, so I have to make sure Ethan never questions... well," he said, glancing over at his son, "where he belongs and where he knows I'll always want him, no matter how his mom's life might change."

"It's good that you're putting him first."

"I have to. I've learned a lot about what matters," Maddox said. "I know life on Christmas Island never seems to change, but sometimes...people do." He wanted to tell her how much he had changed. She could judge the person he'd been years ago all she wanted, but he wasn't entirely that person anymore. Fatherhood had brought him maturity and clarity.

Camille looked away from him and stared over the water. The church was close to the harbor and on a slight elevation. Evergreen trees mixed with hardwoods just beginning to change colors for the autumn season. Maddox had never spent the fall or winter away from the island, but he knew Camille had. What did it feel like for her to come back for good? *Was* she back for good?

"People do change," she agreed. "There's no reason to assume either one of us is the same as we were in high school. What did we really know about ourselves or the world when we were still borrowing our parents' cars and asking permission to be out after eleven?"

"We knew what was in our hearts," Maddox said. It was the most natural response, as he remembered knowing he'd loved Camille. However, he realized his mistake as her expression clouded like a summer storm brewing.

"Did you really know what was in your heart?"

He ran a hand through his hair in exasperation. Yes, but it hadn't prevented him from being impulsive and stupid. Controlling his impulses and thinking first was a skill fatherhood had helped him develop. Calling his brother home from college, admitting he needed help and doing everything he could to rescue the family ferry line had also given him endless hours of practice getting his priorities straight.

"What if…" he began.

"What if what?" Camille asked without returning her gaze to his. She continued watching the bright blue water under the clear autumn sky.

He shook his head. The idea was impulsive, and he'd sworn off being reckless long ago. "Never mind. I had a wild thought that needs to stay where it is."

"Where?"

"In my head and in my heart."

Camille turned her eyes to him and stared him down until he felt that saying something reckless was safer than saying nothing and letting her imagine what he was going to say.

"What if we put the past behind us?" he asked.

"I am," Camille said. "I'm moving the family business forward. Getting my own place."

"I don't mean those things. I mean us."

Camille shook her head emphatically and glanced over to Rebecca, who was chatting with the toy store owner. Maddox could tell Camille wished her friend would return and rescue her from this awkward conversation. He had to go ahead and say the words. When would be his next opportunity for a chance alone with Camille?

"There's no us in the present tense," Camille said. "That's in the past."

"Does it have to be?"

"Of course it does. We're not a thing, Maddox, and we haven't been for a long time. You have your son and your businesses. I have my family and my candy empire." She put on a smile and tried to keep her words light, as if she thought he was joking about their relationship.

"If we were just meeting today, what would happen?"

Camille's smile disappeared. "I don't have time for games."

"Think about it for half a minute. I don't deserve much, but maybe thirty seconds of your time," Maddox said.

Camille swallowed, but she didn't object. "Thirty seconds."

"There's something between us, Camille. If that weren't true, you wouldn't make such an effort to avoid me, and I wouldn't feel like there's a train rushing through my chest just saying these words."

He saw Rebecca heading their way holding a brown paper bag.

"Could we start over with a clean slate? You and me, no hurt from the past, just two people who could be…friends if given the chance."

Camille stared at him. "You want to pretend we're just meeting for the first time, no history."

"I know it sounds—"

"Unrealistic?" Camille cut in. "Yes, it does. This island has so much history I'm surprised the weight doesn't sink it. And we can't ignore the past."

"I wasn't planning to ignore it," Maddox said.

"Got it," Rebecca said, holding up the bag.

Maddox saw the relief on Camille's face that her friend had interrupted, and he struggled to smile politely at Rebecca and thank her. It was clear that there was no point in trying to repair his relationship with Camille. She wouldn't forget, and she wouldn't forgive him.

CHAPTER SIX

CARA ROLLED THE window down on her side of the delivery truck. "I'm glad you're driving, and I'm very glad this is the last Halloween shipment. I like candy, but wow. I can't believe how much is in the back of this truck. What if we sink the ferry?"

"I had more in here last week," Camille said. "And I think the ferry only sank about a foot when I rolled on."

Halloween was only ten days away, and most of their candy had already made the trip from the island to the distribution facility on the mainland that Camille had set up. The final shipment was freshly made fudge in seasonal flavors like pumpkin spice and butternut squash. The hundreds of pounds of themed autumn and Halloween fudge would be express mailed from the mainland post office, and then all Camille's attention would be on the upcoming Christmas season.

"Thanks for coming along today," Camille said. "I've dragged the whole family into my expansion plans."

"You're the boss now, and it's fun delivering candy in this big ugly truck," Cara said. "And if you want to bring me along on your epic candy empire quest, I'll be supportive. You're still my easiest-to-get-along-with sister."

Camille laughed. "Poor Chloe."

Cara groaned. "Poor Chloe, who is pouring more creativity and energy into her wedding than she did for the last seven years running the candy store. She's actually trying to decide on the shade of red for her fingernails and whether or not the bridesmaids should have the same shade."

"That would be funny if we were talking about someone else's Christmas wedding," Camille said. "But we're along for the whole romantic sleigh ride."

"Poor Mom. She's trying to plan the wedding of the century while also doing triple-time on the candy production," Cara said. "I'm glad they turned the future over to you, but they might not have been pre-pared for your energy and very big ideas."

Guilt twisted Camille's stomach. "I'm sorry," she said. "I'm asking a lot of every-one."

"It's in our best interest," Cara said. "If you've looked closely at the returns from the past five years, there's been a modest but definite decline each year. People spend their money on souvenirs and alcohol, but not quite as much on fudge. It gets harder to keep up every summer."

Camille gripped the steering wheel even though the delivery truck's parking brake was on as the ferry took them across the lake. "I keep questioning myself since I've been home. I haven't done that in years, and it's one of the reasons I wanted to get off the island back when I was eighteen."

Cara reached across and nudged her elbow. "Knock it off with the middle-child stuff. That's ancient history."

"I know." Camille sighed. "And that's not really it. I just hope I'm doing the right thing for Island Candy and Fudge."

She watched the seagulls sweep past the ferry hoping for a handout from one of the passengers standing at the railing. Maddox May was in the pilothouse behind her, and if she looked in the side mirror at just the right angle, she could see his outline at the ferry's control panel.

"What else is bothering you?" Cara asked. "And don't say you're concerned about the color of your bridesmaid shoes. Chloe will make that monumental decision for you."

Camille laughed. "Thank goodness."

"Is it Maddox?"

Camille let out a long breath and took her hands off the wheel. She drew a knee beneath her and turned sideways on the seat. "A little. At the craft festival, he made what sounded like a really odd suggestion."

"He offered to let you boil him in a vat of fudge as payback for cheating on you?"

"No."

"Oh, well," Cara said. "It would have ruined the fudge anyway. So what was the suggestion?"

"He wanted to basically erase the past."

Cara nodded. "Excellent idea. That's what you want, too, right?"

"No," Camille blurted. "You can't do that."

"Why not?"

"Because it's…part of who you are. It makes you…you."

Cara frowned. "So I'm a baby sister candy girl all my life?"

"Of course not," Camille said.

"Then…when exactly do you cut off the past?"

Camille stared at her sister. When had Cara gotten so wise?

"You tell me," Camille said.

"That's easy. You chop off the parts you didn't like." She made a chopping motion with her hands. "And you keep all the good stuff. I think that's what the island historians have done, because you never read about the yucky parts of Christmas Island's past like the lack of sanitation services, typhoid outbreaks, bitter feuds between people who felt they had a greater claim to parts of the island. No one wants to think about the garbage ferry that leaves every Sunday morning when everyone's still asleep, but I think we can all agree it's a good thing."

"So you just decide to keep what you want," Camille said.

"Why not? It's your life. You get to choose what luggage you're taking with you. You choose what you forgive and what can still hurt you."

Camille shook her head. "Forgetting the past is a dangerous thing."

"Why? Are you afraid you might fall in love with Maddox May all over again and get your heart broken?"

Camille flinched as if she'd been burned.

"Sorry," Cara said. "Too direct?"

"Ouch," Camille said.

"This is why I hang around with horses instead of people. If I say the wrong thing, they just wait for me to stop talking and give them an apple."

Camille stared through the windshield. The shoreline was coming into focus. Was it possible that she could manage her… issues…with Maddox by controlling them? What if she did agree to turn off the past and begin again with her relationship with him? It would mean she wouldn't be dragged down by the weight of his betrayal. She could treat him as if he was just another Christmas Islander.

It would help her bolster the wall she'd

built between the past and present by taking away the power of the past. She wouldn't have to dread seeing him and wait for the inevitable catch in her breath at the sound of his voice. She could pretend he was just a guy she didn't really know that well. He wouldn't have power over her feelings anymore.

"I think I have an apple in my purse if that helps," Cara said. "It's a peace offering for running my big mouth."

"You don't need to make a peace offering," Camille said. "I was just thinking that maybe you're right."

Cara blew out a breath. "Every little sister loves hearing that, but seriously, don't take my advice if it's stupid. I just want you to move past any trash from your past that could hold you back so you can transform Island Candy and Fudge and take your rightful position as the crown-jewel daughter of the Peterson family. It takes the pressure and attention off me."

Camille looked in the side mirror of the truck and saw Maddox leaning out of the door of the pilothouse to talk to one of his crew members. The sun shone off his dark hair, and he looked handsome and capable. She should continue to view him as though through a side mirror.

The ferry bumped the dock, and Camille released the parking brake, waiting for her turn to drive off the boat—with a lot more confidence than the first time in the truck. She was capable of doing new things and making big plans, and maybe she needed to start by rooting out anything slowing her down.

She watched in her side mirror as Maddox descended the pilothouse stairs two at a time and approached her truck.

"After that silver Buick," he said, pointing to one of the other vehicles on the ferry.

"Got it," she said. She smiled and gave him a thumbs-up, and the hint of surprise that crossed his face made her think she was finally in the driver's seat in their relationship.

CHAPTER SEVEN

SOMETHING WAS DIFFERENT, but Maddox was afraid to think too deeply about it or, worse, test it. Camille stood outside her family's candy store with a huge basket of treats for the Halloween parade. Although Christmas was the island's main commodity, Halloween got a lot of attention, too, as sort of a warm-up or soft opening to the stacked-up holiday season. Thanksgiving was Act II of the play, and Christmas was the grand finale. The autumn season was exhausting but fun.

"I love your costume," Hadley said as Maddox and Ethan stopped outside the Holiday Hotel to pick up candy. Hadley had graduated from the island school with his brother, Griffin, and worked for them at the Holiday Hotel. "But I would never have known who you were if you weren't with this guy," she said, pointing at Maddox.

Ethan put up his hands and roared, fulfilling his mission as a dinosaur, and Hadley stepped back and covered her eyes with her hands. "Too scary," she said. "Take all the candy."

Ethan laughed. "I only want one, so there's enough for the other kids."

Hadley opened her eyes. "You're the sweetest dinosaur I ever saw. And you're getting two pieces of candy just because." She dropped two full-size candy bars in the bucket Maddox carried for his son, and she moved on to the next group of kids.

"I did trick or treat with Mom last year, but it wasn't as much fun. Most of the houses on our street didn't have their lights on, and Mom didn't want me to get much candy anyway," Ethan said.

"I'm sure she just didn't want you to get a tummy ache," Maddox said. For all the faults in their marriage, he refused to make Jennifer a villain. Ethan was the world's best kid, and Maddox knew he couldn't take all the credit. "Ready to cross the street and go down the sidewalk on the other side?"

Maddox knew this would bring them

squarely in contact with Camille, but she'd already been friendly to his son. Her behavior on the ferry the previous week had been friendly, too, and he'd seen her at the post office three days earlier. She'd asked how his day was going, smiled pleasantly and moved through the door as if she wasn't running away from burning lava, like she usually did when he was nearby.

Had the ice started to melt?

He and his son approached Island Candy and Fudge, stopping first at the kite shop next door, where the old man who owned it handed out coloring books and crayons instead of candy.

"Kite pictures," Ethan said, delighted with the gift.

"When you finish coloring one, you can tear it out and bring it back and I'll hang it up right behind the register where everyone can see," the old man said.

Ethan smiled. "Thank you."

They moved toward Camille, who seemed to be waiting for them. "Maddox May, you might want to be careful, because there's a really scary dinosaur following you."

Maddox put a hand over his heart. "If I

stand really still, do you think it won't see me and take a bite out of me?"

Camille laughed, and Ethan popped out from behind Maddox. "I'm a nice dinosaur."

"Now I see that," Camille said. "What kind of treat would a nice dinosaur like?" she asked, tipping her big basket of candy forward so Ethan could see inside.

"Are you going on the hayride later?" Maddox asked as Ethan chose a treat.

Camille nodded. "I am. I've missed those fun things. Can you believe I haven't been on a wagon since I left the island when we graduated?"

Maddox was tempted to hold his breath. Camille had just brought up the dangerous subject between them, but she didn't seem bothered by it. She'd mentioned their high school graduation as if she was talking about the weather.

"Is your sister driving a wagon?" he asked.

Camille laughed. "Cara, you mean? Chloe will make a pillow throne on the back of the wagon, but Cara will have the reins in her hands. She's got five wagons lined up, and I promised her I would choose hers."

"We'll see you there," Maddox said.

"Okay." Camille smiled cheerfully, and Maddox took his son's hand and walked on to the next storefront.

"She's a nice lady," Ethan said as they walked away. Maddox smiled. He thought so, too, but he didn't want to allow himself to hope that Camille was letting go of her anger at him. It seemed too good to be true, and it was only step one. Forgiving him would be nice, but friendship was too much to hope for.

Two hours later as evening descended, the horse barns in the center of the island were illuminated with light and excitement. Strings of orange pumpkin lights lit up the steps onto the wagons, which were also decorated for the occasion.

"Let's go on the skeleton wagon," Ethan said, pointing to one with white plastic skeletons jiggling cheerfully with the movement of people boarding the wagons. Maddox remembered being a kid and going on the hayrides with his family. One year, Flora Winter had ridden along, and there was a variety of islanders every Halloween. Maddox had missed a few years, but he doubted he'd miss any while Ethan was with him.

Maddox saw Cara Peterson on the driver's bench of a pumpkin-themed wagon, and he knew Camille would be on that one. He wanted to sit next to her, as they had in high school, but that was a dangerous move to make now that she was finally warming up to him. He also had his son's wishes to consider, and he would always put Ethan first, no matter what.

Camille climbed onto her sister's wagon with Chloe and her fiancé. She looked over and caught Maddox's eye, but then she plopped down a bright pink pillow for Chloe and joined Cara on the bench seat, where Cara would handle the horses.

Maddox hoisted Ethan onto the skeleton wagon and was stepping up himself when he heard a loud gasp. He snapped his attention to the side of the pumpkin wagon, where a little girl about the same age as Ethan had slid out the side rails and had her foot wedged between the two rear wheels of the wagon. The girl's father was turned around taking care of a younger child, who was fussing about something, and he clearly didn't realize his older child was in trouble.

"Everybody ready to roll?" Cara asked.

"No," Maddox shouted. "Don't move, Cara!"

He told Ethan to stay in his seat, and then he jumped off his wagon and ran to the stuck girl. He didn't know the little girl. Was she a visitor to the island? Her princess costume was tangled in the wheel, and her crown had slipped over her eyes. His shout drew everyone's attention, especially Camille's. She was suddenly above him on the wagon helping the little girl's dad hold her up while Maddox freed her foot.

"Okay," he said to Camille and the girl's father, "you can pull her up or just let her slide through the rails and I'll catch her." The dad pulled the girl up, and Maddox smiled at him. "I would have chosen that, too. Is she about six? I have a son the same age."

The man nodded. "I turned my back for a second—"

"I understand," Maddox says. "Things happen fast."

"I'm new on the island," the man said,

holding out his hand. "Luke Byrnes. I just got hired as a maintenance supervisor at the Great Island Hotel, and everyone said I should bring the girls to this hayride. My wife's home with our baby."

"Maddox May," Maddox said, shaking hands. He was conscious of Camille watching him closely and listening to every word he said. "I own the ferry line and a hotel."

"Is everyone okay?" Cara asked. "Do you think we can get going so we don't hold up the other wagons?"

"I believe so," Camille said.

The island newcomer smiled. "Thanks, Maddox. I owe you. Do you want to join us on our wagon?"

"I'd love to," he said with a glance at Camille. "But my son is waiting for me on the skeleton wagon, and I don't want to disappoint him."

"Are you coming, Dad?" Ethan yelled, right on cue.

"See?" Maddox said.

"That's Ethan," the little girl said, her earlier fright apparently forgotten. "I met him at school already." She waved at Ethan, who waved enthusiastically back.

"Dad, can I come over?" Ethan yelled.

Maddox smiled. "Maybe we'll join you, after all." He glanced up at Camille and Cara. "Would you hold the wagon for one minute?"

He dashed over, helped his son down the steps of the skeleton wagon and hoisted him up on the pumpkin one instead. Ethan sat next to the girl, and they put their heads together and giggled. When Maddox looked up at Camille, she was watching the kids, and then her gaze swung to him and he was sure she was thinking the same thing he was. He and Camille had grown up friends on the island, bonded over dozens of little things. And where were they now?

CHAPTER EIGHT

CAMILLE, HER SISTERS and her mother ran from the car into the bridal salon. The early-November rain and wind storm had given them a rough ferry crossing. Griffin had piloted the boat as safely as the conditions allowed, but he'd warned them they might get stuck on the mainland for the night.

"Should've canceled," Cara grumbled to Camille as they shook off their coats and hung them in the foyer of the dress shop. "We could be warm and dry right now."

"We would have had to reschedule, so we might as well get this over with before November gets any colder," Camille said. "Besides, I can't wait to try on my dress. Christmas red with a green sash, right?"

Cara laughed and rolled her eyes as they followed their mother and Chloe into the back of the salon. Chloe popped into a dressing room, and Camille sat in the elegant wing chairs with her mother on one side and Cara on the other, waiting for the show.

"This is so exciting," her mom said. "My first daughter getting married. I can't wait for your wedding and Cara's."

"You might have to wait awhile," Cara said, leaning forward and giving her mother two raised eyebrows. "You know I prefer horses to people. Speaking of which, if we get stuck on the mainland today, my saddle horses will worry about me."

"Your dad said he'd feed them for you," her mother said. "Besides, we'll get home. Griffin said his brother was on the ferry later today, and he's more willing to take chances."

"You say that like it's a good thing," Camille muttered. She and Cara exchanged a glance, but Camille ignored the twinge she usually got when she heard Maddox's name. She was starting fresh with him, as if they were strangers. He'd figure it out.

Chloe emerged from the dressing room as if she were clothed in a billowing flock of white swans. Her gown had a fitted white bodice with thousands of tiny sparkling sequins. Long lace sleeves extended over the tops of her hands, and the embedded sequins in the lace shimmered. A wide satin sash in Christmas red accented her tiny waist, and then the full white satin skirt cascaded to the floor around her as if she were standing at the top of a tulle-covered mountain.

"Wow," Camille breathed.

"I know," Chloe said. There were tears in her eyes as she waited for her audience's reaction, and her voice was choked with emotion.

"Maybe I will get married someday," Cara said. "If I get to look like that."

"I was just thinking that," Camille said, and then they all laughed.

Camille looked at her mother, who wasn't saying anything, but her feelings were clear in the happy tears running down her cheeks.

She approached her sister and put her hands on both her arms. "I'd hug you, but I'm afraid I'd step on the hem or pop off a sequin, and that dress is absolutely perfect just as it is."

"Mom and Cara and I picked it out last February when I first got engaged, but I didn't want to ruin the surprise by showing you a picture."

"It's perfect," Camille said. "And the fit is just right."

"This is the final fitting, and I don't think it needs any more adjustments," their mother said as she inspected the waistband and then stooped to peer at the hemline.

"I don't want to take it off," Chloe said, "but it's your turn to try on your dresses. I think you're going to love them."

"Hope so. It's only seven weeks until the wedding," Cara said. She'd tried her dress on last spring, and Camille had had Violet take her measurements earlier in the summer and had sent them to the wedding boutique.

"One way to find out," Chloe said. "But don't come out of the dressing room until I get this off. I want to see the big reveal."

For a moment, Camille regretted turning down a few opportunities over the summer to visit the bridal salon. She'd been busy with the family business, and she wasn't sure she wanted to get overly caught up in the wedding hysteria. Balancing her complicated emotions of being back on Christmas Island, claiming her place as the future leader of the candy business and confronting an ex-boyfriend had been plenty for her to handle.

Now it was time to handle this gracefully and be happy for her sister.

"Ready or not," she said, smiling. She and Cara ducked into a large dressing room and helped each other on with their dresses, pulling the long zippers up in the back and being careful not to catch the delicate red satin on either side.

"I'm dreading the green sash," Camille said.

Cara laughed. "We were kidding about that! Just teasing you because you didn't want to come see the dresses for yourself."

Camille turned to the mirror. The bridesmaid dresses were similar to Chloe's, with the fitted bodice and long lace sleeves, but they didn't have sequins, and their skirts were only a fraction of the volume of the bride's. These dresses were made for a holiday celebration, but they weren't over-the-top.

"I'm almost disappointed," she said.

"But I'll console myself by wearing this gorgeous dress and whatever shoes Chloe has already picked out."

"Surprise number two," Cara said. "You get to choose your own shoes. As long as they're black. Now we have to go out there and show Mom and Chloe how these fit. If we do it fast, we might make it back on the ferry before the weather gets worse."

WHEN TOURIST SEASON ended around Halloween, the island ferry ran twice a day, morning and night, until the frozen lake stopped it. Maddox watched the lake from the dock office with one hand on his golden retriever's head.

"No way, Skipper. Right?"

Skipper groaned. The dog was a seasoned voyager, but even he could see it was foolish to cross the lake for only a single group of people. A special group, though, and Maddox was tempted to take a chance. Christmas Islanders would do anything to help each other out, and he'd made exceptions and special trips with the ferry before when a fellow islander needed it.

He would have done it today, but he

knew that getting across safely didn't necessarily mean a safe return voyage. Although his son was happily having dinner and playing board games with Dorothy for the evening, Maddox needed to return home for bath and bedtime.

He needed to get Camille's family home safely, too, but it would have to wait until morning. All he had to do was make the call letting her know they'd be stuck on the mainland tonight.

"I could go," Griffin said behind Maddox. "Rebecca will understand if I miss dinner—as long as I call her first."

Maddox shook his head. "If it's not safe for me, it's not safe for you. Or anyone."

Griffin stood next to his brother, and they watched the wind and waves together. Wind shook the small ticket office, but Maddox knew the windows were sealed tight. It had withstood far worse.

"I believe there were only four return tickets booked, and we can notify them by phone that the ferry's not running," Maddox said.

"Do you want me to make the call?" Griffin asked.

"No. It's my responsibility."

Griffin nodded. "They're islanders. They'll understand."

His brother didn't have to say anything more, because Maddox understood exactly what he meant by that assessment. Living on an island meant you accepted the good with the bad, and the bad sometimes meant being cut off by weather. Not everyone was made for island life. He'd known of several people who'd bought homes on Christmas Island with the intention of getting away from the world and living in what they thought would be an idyllic paradise. And then they endured their first winter, or a medical issue, or even the small daily inconveniences of limited shopping and supplies. Some people embraced the lifestyle and stayed, and others sold out and boarded the ferry a final time.

Maddox took his phone from his pocket and pulled up Camille's number. Had she kept the same number she'd had as a teen? He still had her text messages from a very different time in their relationship. He'd reread those messages the summer she left without a backward glance, and then he'd forgotten about them and focused on making his marriage and his new family work. He'd had two new phones since then, but he'd transferred his contacts and messages over without looking at them.

Was it time to open those old messages? It would be nothing fancy. Quick messages about where and when to meet up after school, her comments on what had happened that day in the candy shop, his descriptions of events on the ferry crossings. Conversations among friends who'd known each other their entire lives. But then those messages had turned emotional, personal. Three little words had begun showing up.

Those messages would bring back all the feelings they'd had and lost. The seven-year gap since the last message spoke volumes about the gulf between them, but was he wrong in thinking that gap might be narrowing?

"Good luck," Griffin said. "And if you want the advice of your big brother, you're making the right choice."

"About the ferry?"

"About your priorities. I know you want to patch up your relationship with Camille now that she's come back to stay, and you're risking her wrath by stranding her on the mainland."

"I think she'll understand about the weather." Maddox shrugged, trying to release the tension in his shoulders. "And about patching up our relationship, I'm not sure that's possible."

"No one can hold a grudge forever on an island. It's not practical to go around hating someone's guts when you're probably going to run into that person at least once a day," Griffin said.

"So my goal is to have her not hate me?"

Griffin grinned. "It's a low bar, but I think you can pull it off."

"What if…" Maddox broke off, not unwilling to confide in his brother but also not sure how to say what was on his mind.

"What if you have a slightly more ambitious goal?" Griffin supplied.

"I guess."

Griffin sat on the corner of the ticket office desk. Maddox remembered dozens of conversations with their father in that office during the long winters when they all dreamed of getting out on the blue lake under the summer sun. With their father's death, Maddox had grown closer to Griffin. They relied on each other and shared the same dream for their family business. Griffin had found someone to love in Rebecca, and Maddox had his son, with his sweet smile and unconditional love. But the two brothers shared a bond and could almost read each other's thoughts.

"I'm a huge fan of second chances," Griffin said.

It had been a long time since Maddox and his brother had spoken about the way he'd messed up his relationship with Camille. Did Griffin think there might be a second chance for Maddox and Camille?

"In theory," Griffin added. "In practice, it doesn't seem logical to go down that road unless something has really changed."

"Or someone," Maddox said, feeling deflated that Griffin wasn't offering encouragement in the Camille direction.

"I'll give you that," Griffin said. He smiled. "You're the same old chump, but Camille seems like a new woman. Full of confidence and plans, finally free of Chloe's shadow."

Maddox was stunned. "You see that, too, huh?" Maddox had thought only he recognized the change in her because he knew Camille so well, even now.

"Not at first, but then Rebecca filled me in a bit. It's not easy being the younger sibling of someone so perfect," he said, giving his brother a light punch on the upper arm. "You should know."

"Go home to the mansion Aunt Flora left you," Maddox said, smiling and shaking his head. "Leave the dirty work of running the business to me for the day."

"Finally," Griffin said. He pulled on his waterproof coat and zipped it all the way to his chin. "Camille isn't the only one who has changed," he said seriously. "You've added a few layers."

"Good layers?"

"Yes. Good luck disappointing Camille."

Maddox tried to smile. "At least I have a good reason this time."

"Your son needs you to come home safely, and I don't want you to scuff up our boat," Griffin said. "Very good reasons."

After his brother left, Maddox debated on a phone call or a text. Would his number still be in Camille's phone after all these years, or would his call come up as an unknown number?

She answered on the second ring.

"Hello, Maddox."

That answered his question, and he momentarily forgot the words he'd rehearsed to break the bad news to her about the ferry. She hadn't erased him. Did she ever review those old messages?

"Hi," he said. "Camille, I'm sorry, but the weather—"

"I know. It's okay. I wouldn't ask you to take a risk if it's just for us."

Although he'd known she would understand, he also heard the disappointment in her voice. Or was it something else? Worry? Tension?

"You're important," he said.

"It's okay," she repeated. "I'm going to take this opportunity to show Mom and Chloe the building I'm using for distribution, and then we'll crash at her fiancé Dan's house and have a girls' night."

"That sounds great," Maddox said.

"Which part?" she asked.

He smiled at the trace of humor in her voice.

"Girls' night. It's been a while for me," he said.

Camille laughed. "Honestly, me, too. We tried on dresses and shoes and jewelry, so we might as well hunker down with a bottle of wine and a jar of nail polish."

"Does Dan know you might be coming?"

"Chloe is on the phone with him right now. He has a four bedroom house he lives in by himself right now, so we'll be fine."

"I'll be over first thing in the morning to rescue you."

After he said it, he wished he hadn't used the word *rescue*. It sounded too dramatic, even romantic. He was the one who had destroyed their relationship, so talking about saving Camille from anything was a stretch.

"Thank you," Camille said as if she was talking to person who had just delivered her pizza. "We'll be ready." She ended the call, and Maddox set the phone next to him on the ticket desk. The stormy gray afternoon was already turning into night, and he was tempted to indulge in memories of a time when his life had been simpler. His father had made the tough calls about the weather, and his family drifted from day to day running the business that he'd vaguely thought he might take over when he grew up.

That day had come much faster than he'd imagined, and he had a son waiting for him in the home where he'd taken his own first steps and lost his first tooth. He needed to get home to Ethan. They'd skip the wine and nail polish, but maybe he and his son would have a guys' night. They could watch a movie and have microwave popcorn. Maybe they'd both put on their pajamas and share a blanket as the November rain fell outside.

Camille was his past, but Ethan was his future. Like everything else on the island, the past and future blended together. He'd lost focus once on where his path to happiness lay, and he knew he could never go back and change what he did to Camille. But he would also never take his eyes off what mattered again.

CHAPTER NINE

CAMILLE BUNDLED UP and rode her bike the short distance from her downtown apartment to her parents' house. It was early morning on the mid-November day, and her hands froze inside her fleece gloves. She pedaled quickly, because she couldn't be late for a special breakfast.

"Double birthday time," Camille's mother said as she dropped dough circles into frying oil in the kitchen. "And I'm making you and your dad's favorite doughnut recipe."

"Can I help?" Camille asked as she shed her coat and gloves.

"No," her mother said, turning a smile on her. "You shouldn't have to work on your birthday at twenty-six or fifty-six."

"I'll remember that when I'm fifty-six," Camille said. She pulled out a kitchen chair and sat at her place, where there was already a pink envelope and little gift-wrapped box next to her coffee cup.

"Can't believe your father is that old today," her mother said. "He seems just as young as the day he was lucky enough to meet me."

Camille laughed. "Best day of his life." She knew the story her mother was about to tell, and she sat back, ready to enjoy it again. Family folklore and stories were the good parts of belonging to a tight-knit clan. If her sisters were in the room, they might exchange a good-humored eye roll, but none of them really minded.

"That's what I always tell him. It was a good thing his eighteenth birthday was a beautiful day and his parents took him to Lakeside for a birthday lunch. It was only my second week working as a waitress at the restaurant, and my parents didn't like me working there. They wanted me to be a journalist or a doctor."

Her mother paused with a pair of tongs as she waited to flip the frying doughnuts. "Can you imagine if I'd never brought him his Reuben with fries and we'd never met?"

Camille got up and poured her coffee cup full. "Do you think he'd be running his family's candy empire all alone, wishing a beautiful brunette who shared his passion for candy would come along and scan the distant shore every night as the sun set and the stars came out?"

"Heaven forbid," her mother said. "I'm sure some island girl or visitor would have snapped him up if I hadn't."

"Are you telling the birthday lunch story again?" Camille's father, Ron, asked as he stuck his head around the kitchen doorway. "And, more importantly, do I smell dough-nuts and cinnamon?"

"Hot out of the fryer," her mother said as she sprinkled the steaming doughnuts with cinnamon sugar. "And your daughter was being dramatic and adding to the story."

"Chloe's not up yet, is she?" he asked.

Camille and her mother laughed.

"Take these," her mother said as she gave a blue plate of doughnuts an extra shake of the cinnamon sugar and put it on her dad's place mat. "Happy birthday to my sweet-heart."

Her mom and dad kissed lightly on the lips and smiled at each other. "Reubens for lunch?" he asked.

"Always."

Camille's dad picked up two doughnuts and put them on a plate, which he slid in front of Camille as he brushed a kiss over her cheek. "Happy birthday, honey."

"And happy birthday to you, too," she said. "Am I your best birthday present again this year?"

"Every year."

"Even the year I accidentally opened your presents and cried when I got a wallet and a circular saw?"

"Especially that year. I was very excited about that saw, and I didn't have to go to the trouble of unwrapping it. Not to mention my relief when I realized the pink ice skates were for you."

Those ice skates still hung on a peg in her bedroom upstairs. They hadn't fit in years, but she couldn't give them up because of all the happy memories of skating in them. She'd jammed her feet into them one season too long and ended up with blisters, but just the sight of them brought back the feeling of spinning in circles on a frozen cove on the north side of the island. A group of islanders had held hands and made a chain, and Maddox was right behind her tugging at her mitten and trying to snap the whole chain and make them fall.

He'd been reckless and unpredictable as a boy, riding his bike right to the edge of the island cliffs or going out into the water way beyond where his toes could touch bottom. The weekend before, when he'd canceled the ferry because of the weather, Camille had been a little surprised. Would the Maddox she'd grown up with have canceled the trip or used it as an opportunity to prove himself against the elements? Or prove himself to her?

Either way, he'd made that call and put everyone's safety first. Declined to rescue her, as he'd put it, but she liked the maturity it demonstrated. And she hadn't needed rescuing. Dan's home was large and elegant, and Chloe enjoyed hosting what she called her first party in what would be her new home. Camille and her sisters and mom had taken advantage of the extra time on the mainland to get some shopping done.

"We were lucky to get stuck in Lakeside last weekend, because I went to the big sporting goods store and got you something special," Camille said.

"I would rather have had you home that night," he said. "I wanted you to be safe, but this house was very lonely."

Camille laughed. "You mean it was quiet. And wait until you see what I got you. That lonely night was probably worth it."

Her dad closed his eyes and crossed the fingers of both hands. "Fishing pole, fishing pole, fishing pole," he chanted.

"You saw the shape of the package, didn't you?" Camille asked.

He opened his eyes. "Am I right?"

"You'll have to be surprised when Chloe and Cara get downstairs and we open presents. After that, I'm taking the truck across on the morning ferry to deliver another batch of Christmas candy."

"On your birthday?" her mother asked.

"It has to be done, and Mondays are good days to deliver to the post office. The candy won't have to sit over a weekend waiting to be shipped out."

"You work too hard," her mother said as she dropped another doughnut on Camille's plate.

"Thank you," Camille said. Her mother probably thought she was saying thank you for the doughnut, but it was also for her mother's words. Of course she worked hard. It was the only way to get what she wanted and make sure she'd earned it. Things that were easy or came about through luck could be just as easily yanked away. Maddox had been so easy to fall in love with. It was the one thing in her life she hadn't had to fight for or work toward. And look what had happened to that.

"Do you need me to come along today?" her father offered.

"No way," her mother said. "You're not missing your traditional birthday lunch."

Her father exchanged a glance with Camille, and she heard her sisters giggle as they came into the kitchen. The three daughters all knew their dad's secret—that he hated Reubens and had ordered one accidentally that day he turned eighteen. But he'd never been brave enough to ruin it for their mother, so he choked down a sandwich every year. Cara had once pointedly asked him why he didn't just come out and tell his wife the truth, and Camille would never forget his answer. *When you love someone*, he'd said, *it's not about you anymore, it's about both of you.*

Camille had just started seriously dating Maddox at the time and she'd taken the words to heart, believing that all their future decisions, traditions and even secrets would be about them, not just her. Since that disaster, Camille had decided to put herself first instead of taking chances on falling in love again.

"Girls," her mother said, addressing Cara and Chloe, "talk Camille out of working on her birthday."

"Take the day off," Chloe said cheerfully. "I always took my birthday off when I was running the store. You can't work all the time."

"I enjoy working," Camille said. She wanted to add that hard work was necessary if you wanted the family business to grow instead of remaining pleasantly stagnant.

"Life is about more than just work," her mother said. "Which is something you're going to have to learn if you want to be happy."

Camille didn't like arguing with her parents, and especially not on her birthday, but she already had her day mapped out. And she was perfectly happy. Sitting around her apartment for the sake of taking a day off wouldn't get her where she needed to be.

MADDOX KNEW THE DATE. He'd thought of her when he saw the date on his watch just as he had for years. November 15. Camille's family always sent in the best birthday treats for the entire school when a candy girl had a birthday. He used to know Cara's and Chloe's birthdays, too, but he'd forgotten them over the years.

Maddox couldn't forget Camille's.

He was getting ready for the morning trip across to the mainland when he saw Camille's rented refrigerated truck lumbering down Holly Street toward the ferry entrance.

The woman was nonstop.

He strode over and greeted her before she got out of the truck to pay her passage with Dorothy at the ticket window.

"No charge today," he said.

Camille cocked her head. "Isn't the ferry running?"

"Sure it is. It's a beautiful day. But it's your birthday," Maddox said.

Camille's mouth opened, and she stared at him without speaking.

"It's November 15, isn't it?" he asked.

She nodded.

Maddox wanted to reach for her hand where it rested on the open window frame, but he didn't. "Did you think I would forget?" he asked.

"People forget important things all the time," she said. "And the birthday of an acquaintance isn't exactly important."

"We're not just acquaintances," he said. No matter that they hardly spoken a hundred sentences since their breakup, there was no way to reduce their childhood and teenage years to just casual friendship. It would always be more than that.

Camille drummed her fingers lightly on the window frame, and Maddox waited. When he was around her, he felt as if he was in his sock feet trying not to make noise as he advanced slowly toward something he wished he could have. He nodded toward her silver necklace. "Was that a birthday gift?"

Camille touched the silver candy cane on a chain. "From my parents. It's very appropriate for a former candy girl."

"You're still a candy girl, but now you're calling the shots," Maddox said.

Camille dropped her hand. "It's my dad's birthday, too," she said.

"I remember that."

"I got him a fishing pole when we were stranded in Lakeside last weekend."

"He may have to wait until next spring to use that," Maddox said. "But it gives him something to look forward to. Winters can be pretty long here."

"I know. This will be my first one in quite a while, and I hope I…well, I hope I still remember how."

Maddox swallowed. This was the closest they'd come to breaking through a layer of surface ice in the months since she'd returned to the island. He didn't want to shatter the moment.

Skipper padded over and jumped up to put his front paws on the truck's door. Camille laughed and reached out to touch his golden paw. Church bells from the steeple on the hill above town signaled the time as Camille took her gaze from the dog and looked Maddox in the eye.

"We should get going," she said.

"You're my only passenger."

"And I don't have a ticket yet."

"You don't need one. This ride is free," he said.

"But—"

"It's your birthday."

Camille smiled. "You don't have to do that."

"I want to," he said. He backed away before he said more than he should. "Go ahead and pull into the middle—balance the weight that way."

She nodded.

"Camille?" he asked. "Is your mom making your dad eat the Reubens he hates today?"

He remembered Camille confiding that story to him when they were in love. She'd promised him she would never make him eat something he hated, and he'd given her a list of things he disliked. They'd made a joke of it, and she'd also given him a list of foods she found loathsome.

"I'm missing out on that glorious lunch,"

she said. Her eyebrows drew together, and instead of the smile he expected at the memory, she looked terribly sad. Was she sorry she was missing lunch with her family on a special occasion in order to make a candy delivery?

"Did you ever learn to like marshmallows?" she asked. "I thought of you every time I…"

She didn't finish her sentence, but she didn't have to. She'd thought of him. She remembered something he'd shared with her. And the expression on her face made it clear that remembering all they'd shared made her so sad she wouldn't even finish her sentence.

"S'mores are still my nightmare," he said, and he was glad when her expression relaxed into a smile as she drove onto the ferry. He would gladly eat a bag of marshmallows if it could bring him and Camille closer together, but he had to rely on time to take small bites out of the pain he'd caused them both.

CHAPTER TEN

"I SHOULD WALK," Camille said. "You know we're all going to overeat."

"Get in," her mother said. "It's freezing."

Camille ducked through the sliding door on the side of the family minivan and got in the closest seat. Both her sisters were crammed in the middle seat, too, and their parents were in the front, just as they had been when Camille was growing up. The van was only a few years old, purchased while Camille was away, but the three-girls-in-the-back vibe was the same.

Chloe had her legs stretched out in the middle, and the glittery thread in her burgundy velvet tights glimmered in the late-afternoon light. "I like your boots," Camille said, pointing to Chloe's black ankle boots with sparkly stones along the zippers.

"How about me?" Cara asked. "I wore my good barn boots for the special occasion."

"You don't really wear those in the barn, do you?" Camille asked. "They look too nice."

Cara glanced down at her shiny brown leather knee boots. "No."

Camille had selected gray tights with a dressy green sweater and black boots. She'd blown out her long blond hair and let it flow over her shoulders instead of twisting it up and hiding it under a hat or net as she did every day at the candy store. The island Thanksgiving party hosted every year for locals only at the Great Island Hotel was festive but not formal, and Camille felt warm inside just anticipating the massive buffet, autumn decorations and welcoming feeling of the event.

Her dad pulled out from behind her downtown apartment and took the road leading up the hill to the Great Island Hotel. As a child, she'd made this trip, always filled with wonder and anticipation, because the massive hotel was only for rich people, except for the few magical times a year when islanders were welcome.

"Dan is spending Thanksgiving with his family, and he wanted me to come, but I told him I couldn't miss this." Chloe's voice quivered as she spoke. "This could be my last time going to the island Thanksgiving with all of you."

Their mom turned around from the front seat, and Camille saw tears in her eyes. "You can come back every year. Camille went away, but she's back. You can certainly do that, too."

Camille wanted the sad conversation to end quickly before actual tears began flowing, although she did take a second to appreciate the fact that there were a few things she'd managed to do before Chloe. She'd left. And she'd returned.

"I've been thinking about my wedding," Chloe said.

Cara and Camille exchanged a quick glance. Their sister had been thinking and talking about her wedding nonstop. They knew every detail of the three-tiered cake with just the right amount of sparkle topped with an arrangement of red flowers and Christmas greenery.

"Maybe it's a mistake," Chloe added.

The van hitched a little as their father backed off the accelerator and then hit it again when they reached the driveway sloping up to the Great Island Hotel.

"Honey," their mother said, again turning around. "It's a holiday, and it's natural to feel sentimental. It's also natural to feel nervous about making a big change in your life."

"It is a big change," Chloe said. "I'm not sure I can go through with it."

Camille put an arm around her sister. "You love Dan, and it's going to be fine."

Chloe shook her head. "Not all marriages work, especially the ones where the people are literally from different worlds."

The marriage of Maddox and Jennifer swept into Camille's mind. That marriage hadn't worked, but it had also been built on an accidental pregnancy and a desire to do the right thing without, she assumed, a great love involved. Had Maddox loved Jennifer when they got married? Had he grown to love her? She hadn't allowed herself to think about it very much.

"You're not from different worlds," Cara said. "That would be like having your own sun and ecosystem and traveling light-years between galaxies. Dan is from Lakeside, where I'm pretty sure they share our same climate and language."

"You know what I mean," Chloe protested.

Cara's stomach growled. "I know I'm starving and I can't wait to race all of you to the buffet."

"Chloe, honey," their dad said from the front seat. Camille waited. While their dad was a sweet, sympathetic, involved parent, he generally steered around the wreckage of broken hearts and emotional drama. When Maddox had cheated on her at the end of senior year, Camille had cried on her mother's shoulder, and her dad had given her an awkward hug and told her he loved her enough for ten people and Maddox was a fool. It hadn't really helped, but he'd tried.

"I have a suggestion," he continued as he parked at the historic hotel. Of course he somehow managed to park next to Maddox's pickup.

"What if you enjoy the party today and we'll talk about all the wonderful ways you can make your marriage work tomorrow?" their father continued. "Your mother and I can each write a list of fifteen things to do—"

"Or not do," their mother cut in, and all three girls laughed.

"And we can all spend our day off discussing marriage 101. I am, after all, an expert on this, because I married a mainlander," their dad continued. "I'm sure your mother will tell you moving to the island was the best thing that ever happened to her."

Although she tried to be quiet about it, all three girls heard their mother whisper, "Not helping," in the front seat.

Chloe sighed. "Maybe I worry too much. Or maybe Dan should move here instead of me moving there?"

No one said it, but they all knew it wasn't possible for Dan to continue his pediatrics practice on the island. While he visited the island for children's checkups, he didn't need a whole practice there. There just weren't enough children to be served. After Camille had seen his beautiful home on the mainland, she had no concerns about her sister's future well-being, once she got used to the idea and made the initial leap.

Cara tugged open her door. "Let's eat."

On the way to the door, Camille walked with her dad. "Nice try back there."

"I'm not good at the emotional stuff sometimes."

"You're fine. I'm a bit worried about what's going to happen when we get inside, because it's sentimental city."

Her father cut her a curious look. "Sentimental city?"

"I came over earlier today and helped set up a history display. Next summer is the big bicentennial, and Shirley from the Chamber of Commerce already recruited me to do up some kind of island history thing. Maybe a small book or a narrated video or something. Tonight is the launch of the Christmas Island bicentennial, and there are a bunch of sweet and sappy photos of island life that might even make Cara a little teary-eyed."

Her father sighed. "We're in big trouble."

As Camille entered the lobby, she saw Maddox and Ethan wearing matching navy blue sweaters. Maybe she didn't want to think too deeply about island history, either. She also saw her sister's fiancé pop out from behind an ornate pillar holding a bunch of red roses. Chloe rushed to him and hugged him, and the rest of Camille's family walked over to greet him.

"I should have called," Dan said, "but I wasn't sure I could get away until the last minute, and then I decided to surprise you. I was glad to catch the plane before it left Lakeside." He kissed Melinda on the cheek. "Can I hope for a bed at your house tonight?"

"You can have Camille's old room," she said. "She has her own place now, and we'd love to have you."

Camille and Cara exchanged a smile. Now that Chloe had put aside her worries, the rest of the night would be smooth sailing, and they could all enjoy their food.

A group of people were gathered around the history display in the lush lobby of the hotel, and Maddox and Ethan lingered near the replica of a sailing ship perched on a table. Camille followed her family straight into the dining room. The long room had mirrored columns and a wall of windows with an amazing view of the lake. At night, the candlelight gave the massive room a cozy and elegant feel.

Long buffet tables were set up. Vases of autumn flowers in rich yellows and reds contrasted with the white tablecloths, and the aroma of five-star food filled the space. Camille saw Rebecca and Griffin at a table for four and waved.

"Come over and take the table by us," Rebecca said, motioning to a table large enough for Camille's family right next to them. Camille could imagine the other two table occupants were looking at a ship in the lobby. Did she really want to sit next to Maddox at dinner? There was no way to turn down her best friend without being rude, though, and since she had decided to treat Maddox as a casual friend with whom she had no interesting history, she should be fine.

Camille smiled. "Thanks, we'd love to." Her parents took places on the other side of the rectangular table, and Chloe sat on one end. Cara tossed her purse on a remaining chair and took off for the buffet, leaving Camille with the chair closest to

Maddox. She told herself being close to Maddox wouldn't affect her.

"That's a great history display in the lobby," Rebecca said over the sounds of voices and clinking plates and silverware. "And I heard you're the featured speaker tonight."

Camille felt her empty stomach drop. "There's no featured speaker that I know of."

Rebecca cocked her head. "That's not what the programs say." She held out a piece of folded cardstock with embossed gold letters on the front spelling out Christmas Island Thanksgiving Feste. The logo of the Great Island Hotel was embossed in red foil beneath it. Camille slowly opened the paper. On one side was a detailed menu listing out the buffet and dessert items along with select beverages. On the facing page was a one-paragraph summary of the island's history that she had written for the Chamber of Commerce, a reprinted photograph of an early picture of the island and a program note explaining that Camille Peterson would be kicking off the island's bicentennial with some remarks about her historical research into Christmas Island's glorious past.

Camille closed the program and forced a lopsided grin. "I guess I didn't know what I was getting myself into when I was asked to 'help'—" she made air quotes when she used the word "—get ready for the two hundredth anniversary of the island."

"You could probably get yourself proclaimed island historian if you wanted to."

Griffin glanced up from his salad and smiled at her. "I think it does say that next to your name."

Camille opened the brochure again and checked, and then she laughed. "Very funny."

"It won't be long," he said. "This island has a way of grabbing you and not letting go."

"All I did was say I would be on hand to answer any questions about the pictures. And now I believe I'm starring in a Hollywood adaptation of the true history of Christmas Island."

"I hope I'm featured in that as a hero," Maddox said as he walked up with his son.

"Hi, candy lady." Ethan climbed up on

the chair nearest Camille's and hung over the back, smiling at her.

"Hello, Ethan. No candy tonight, but I know from experience there will be wonderful desserts."

The boy had his father's eyes and smile, and seeing him reminded Camille of being a child herself and coming to the Thanksgiving Feste at the Great Island Hotel. Her family had probably sat next to the May family many times, although everyone tended to table hop and visit at the yearly event.

"Ice cream?" Ethan asked.

"Maybe. And cake and pie, too," Camille said.

Maddox picked up his son and deposited him one chair over and then draped his jacket over the back of another chair... right behind Camille's.

As HE ATE, Maddox kept one eye on his son's plate to make sure he wasn't gobbling anything too fast. He'd also placed a mental bet on whether the vegetables would disappear into a napkin. The rest of his attention was behind him. His chair back and

Camille's touched when he scooted back to pick up a fork his son had dropped. Camille's chair had connected with his when she got up to go to the dessert buffet.

He tilted his head and saw her at the dessert table with Rebecca.

"Are you thinking about something sweet?" Griffin asked.

Maddox turned his attention to his brother. "I'm afraid of overdoing it."

"We're having dessert, right?" his son asked.

"You can for sure," he said.

"Rebecca's having Camille over for lunch tomorrow, and then they're going online and taking advantage of all the Black Friday sales from the comfort of the Winter Palace."

"Much better than fighting crowds at the mall," Maddox said.

"What are you doing tomorrow—now that our ferry season has ended?"

Maddox moved his son's water glass so he wouldn't knock it over as he reached for another biscuit from the bread basket. The daily ferry schedule officially ended on Thanksgiving every year, but they would still run a weekend ferry and special trips as requested. In the winter months, travel to and from the mainland shifted to private boat when necessary or via small plane from the island airport. When the lake froze, usually after Christmas, all boat traffic ended for a few months, and daily mail came over on airplanes, too.

"Ethan is helping me with our project at the house," Maddox said. "By springtime, we'll have a basement playroom complete with a pool table and a big screen where we can race cars."

"Santa is bringing me games," Ethan said.

"He's bringing them to both of us and we'll share," Maddox said. "I'm trying to be very good until Christmas."

As he spoke, Camille returned and brushed against him as she took her chair and scooted it up to the table behind him. It was hard being good when he really just wanted to turn around and kiss her. She had started to be friendlier to him. Was it just because she'd decided it was pointless to hate him, or was there a slim chance they could rekindle what they'd once had?

He'd thrown away the love of his life, but could there be a second chance for them?

"Dad, the candy lady put a marshmallow on your plate when you were looking at Uncle Griffin."

Maddox looked down at his plate. There was a mini-marshmallow, the kind that was probably from the hot chocolate bar set up near the dessert bar, on the edge of his plate, as if it had been tossed there.

"She must not know you hate those," his son said.

Maddox was not going to tell his son the candy lady knew very well how he felt about marshmallows. He didn't actually know why she'd put it there—except as some sort of a message or a challenge? Was it a shot across his bow or an invitation to play?

The leader of the island Chamber of Commerce, Shirley, and the owner of the Great Island Hotel, Quentin, moved down the center aisle of the dining room, waving to everyone and capturing the attention of the room as they took the microphone at a small stage. The stage was generally used for a quartet playing dinner music for the hotel's legendary nightly five-course meal, but tonight there was a poster set up on an easel next to the microphone stand.

Quentin welcomed everyone and wished them a happy Thanksgiving. There were several hundred year-round residents of Christmas Island, and Maddox knew they were nearly all there for the Thanksgiving dinner, like usual. He glanced around the room. He'd only missed a few of these occasions when he'd spent the holiday with his ex-wife's family on the mainland. He was glad that his son was attending his first one and would, if things went as planned, continue to make it a tradition.

Shirley took the microphone and gave a speech about the island's bicentennial and plans to reflect on and celebrate the island's past and future. Maddox was hardly paying attention to what she said. Both he and Camille had turned their chairs to face the speaker, and they were seated side by side, their elbows touching. All he could think about was how nice she smelled. Did she still smell of fresh, sweet mint? He'd never been sure if it was her soap or a scent from the candy shop, but he recognized the sweet aroma even over the smells of the Thanksgiving feast.

Maddox wasn't listening to the speaker, but Camille clearly was, because he heard her name and then she rose quickly from her seat and walked to the podium. He watched her bright sweater and long blond hair weave among the tables on the way to the small stage. What was she going to say?

"I never thought when I went off to college to be a history major that I would come back someday and take on a history project on Christmas Island," she said when she took the microphone.

Maddox had somehow managed to forget she'd majored in history. As far as he knew, she'd started working for a candy company after college in Chicago and then had returned to the island to work with her family. He'd skipped college himself, and his brother had put in less than two years before it was necessary for him to come home and help with the family business. Maddox didn't regret missing out on college. He'd learned all his lessons the hard way in the past seven years.

"Of course I love the island and I love

history, so this should be a perfect combination," Camille said, her voice floating out over the dining room. Maddox took his eyes from her face for a moment and looked around. Every person in the world who mattered to him was in that room, and they were all focused on Camille, who had once been his entire world. When he returned his attention to Camille, he caught her eye. Had she been looking at him when his gaze was turned elsewhere?

"I don't want to ruin the surprise for you, or, quite frankly, for myself, since I don't exactly know what our plans are," she said, smiling. "But next summer is the two hundredth anniversary of the island's settlement, and we'll need everyone's help documenting the island history with pictures and stories. If you have pictures or artifacts to be included, you could stop by Island Candy and Fudge." She smiled. "You can't miss it—it's the one with the pink-and-white awning."

Everyone laughed, and Maddox smiled when he heard his son whisper reverently, "I love that place." Ethan didn't get Camille's joke because he didn't yet know that everyone knew everyone else's secrets on the island. Most people could name the carpet color in the living room in each other's houses, knew exactly whose cars were circling the island on the perimeter road and which kids would graduate from high school in the coming months. Ethan didn't know it, but everyone on the island knew the details of his daddy's mistake with the mainland girl and that they were now divorced and working out the custody agreements for the boy's future.

It wasn't a bad thing, Maddox thought as he soaked in the familiar atmosphere of the room. Did Camille feel the same way, happy to be back and wrapped in the warm embrace of the island residents?

Camille finished her speech and there was polite applause, but Maddox hardly heard it. He was watching her as she came back to her seat. There was color in her cheeks. Was it from the attention of the entire room, or did it have anything to do with her meeting his eyes as she moved toward him?

She took her chair and turned it back toward her family, her back to him. But as he looked down at the marshmallow on his plate's edge, Maddox knew that he and Camille had plenty of things they needed to talk about.

CHAPTER ELEVEN

CAMILLE STOOD WITH her friends and family on the wide lawn of the Great Island Hotel. She shivered in the frosty air as they awaited the countdown. The hotel had a reputation for putting up so many outdoor lights that it could be seen as a shining beacon from across the lake in Lakeside. Workers, including local volunteers, spent weeks before Thanksgiving wrapping the trees, porch and architectural details of the century-old structure with thousands of lights in anticipation of the customary lighting ceremony after the Thanksgiving dinner.

"I'll miss this," Chloe said, even though her arm was firmly pulled through Dan's and she didn't look as if she was on the brink of calling off her wedding.

"No, you won't," Cara said. "You can see

the lights from Lakeside, or you can commandeer a boat and join us."

"It won't be the same," Chloe said.

Camille shoulder-hugged her sister. "It could be better. You might not be stuffed to the gills with food and regretting eating so much. Whatever they do to their mashed potatoes should come with an advisory."

"Who are the lighters this year?" Camille's dad asked.

Every year, the youngest person and the oldest person at the dinner put their hands together and pulled the ceremonial switch to turn on all the lights and awe the spectators.

"I wish Aunt Flora had come," Maddox said. "She said it was too cold. It would have been fun to have her and Ethan do it together."

Camille turned. "Is Ethan the youngest person here tonight?"

"Not quite. The new maintenance guy for the hotel has a four-year-old, and she's going to do the honors with the pastor's mother, who's visiting. Still, it would have been great if the timing had worked for Ethan and Flora."

"They can do a mock one at Christmas when Aunt Flora comes," Griffin said.

"She's coming for Christmas?" Camille asked.

Maddox nodded. "We're her family, and she seems to think this could be her last Christmas."

"I hope she's not sick," Camille said.

"Not that we know of, but it will be nice to see her and make sure she has people around her who care about her."

"How about her nephew Alden?"

Maddox shook his head. "I think he's traveling somewhere far away."

Camille knew the story of the previous summer, when Alden had tried to destroy some paperwork he found at the Winter Palace because he thought he was entitled to a greater inheritance from his aunt. When he learned she had left her personal fortune to Griffin and Maddox May and only a sliver of Winter Industries to Alden, he'd left the island in a huff, and no one had seen him since.

"What are you doing for Christmas?" Maddox asked.

"Smiling through my sister's wedding

and then collapsing. It's a big deal, but now that I've seen my dress, I'm feeling better about it."

"You're not a big peppermint drop or a candy cane, are you?"

Camille laughed. "I'll be wearing a very nice red dress. No gumdrop earrings or sugarplum buttons."

"You'll be beautiful," Maddox said.

They'd fallen into friendly conversation just as they would have years earlier. It was pleasant, comfortable and sweet. So it took Camille five seconds to register any shock at his compliment. He used to call her that, used to greet her after school or over the phone with a "hey, beautiful." She opened her mouth to tell him he'd lost the right to talk to her that way when the crowd began the countdown to the official lighting. Beginning with ten and slowly counting down, Camille and Maddox stared at each other until the entire lawn full of their friends and relatives got to five before they broke eye contact.

Maddox knelt down and put an arm around his son, and Camille held her breath for the last few seconds before the world was filled with twinkling lights. Camille heard Maddox tell his son, "I'm thankful for you," and it jogged her memory. It was the island tradition. In the moments after the lights illuminated the trees and the entire front of the Great Island Hotel, islanders turned to each other and named something they were thankful for in honor of the Thanksgiving holiday.

"I'm thankful for three wonderful daughters," Camille's mother said. "And an upcoming wedding."

"I'm thankful for my new fishing pole," her father said with a grin. "And what your mother said."

"Sisters," Chloe said. "And the best future husband. And my beautiful wedding dress that I can't wait to wear."

"No horseflies in the winter," Cara said.

Camille knew it was her turn, and everyone around her was waiting for her. She could think of many reasons to be thankful, but which of them should she say aloud? The fact that people loved candy? Having her own apartment? Perhaps the strange new feeling of ease when she saw Maddox or heard his name. She no longer felt as if she was trying to breathe underwater. Was she finally over him completely, freeing her?

"Look, it's Santa," someone shouted. It drew everyone's attention away from Camille, and the crowd began to move back toward the front porch of the hotel, where Santa appeared, waving.

"Dad," Ethan said.

"Just a second," Maddox said.

Maddox waited, apparently wanting to hear Camille's declaration of thanks even though most people around them, including her family, had gotten distracted by Santa's appearance.

"I've got him," Griffin said, taking Ethan's hand. Rebecca took Ethan's other hand, and they walked toward the porch, leaving Maddox and Camille alone amid the white lights strung overhead on the lawn. A few flakes of snow fell, and Camille brushed one off her nose.

"What were you going to say?" Maddox asked.

"I don't know."

He waited and then reached over and

brushed snow from her hair. The touch was familiar but also new.

"I have so many things I'm thankful for," she said. She'd be lying if she didn't admit that one item on her list was standing right in front of her. When she'd arrived on the island, her plan was to draw a firm line dividing the past from the future. Seal off the past, don't think about it, don't let it weigh you down. She'd thought it was the only way. But she realized something as the trees turned and lost their leaves and the winter calm of the island descended.

She didn't have to wall off the past. It was possible to remember it and treasure the place it held in her life without wanting to relive it or revive it. She was a history major, and rationally she knew that ignoring the past was dangerous.

"I'm thankful I grew up on this island," she said.

Maddox smiled. "Me, too."

"And I'm thankful for all the good things that happened while I was growing up."

Maddox shoved his hands in his pockets and glanced over at the group gathered around the porch, where Santa stood waving and smiling. Camille knew from experience that Santa was making a brief appearance only and would remind all the kids how they should be good and how much he was looking forward to bringing them gifts in a month. She only had a few minutes left alone with Maddox before everyone would notice they weren't by the porch.

"Does that include me?" he asked.

Camille swallowed. "It has to."

"I remember standing out here on nights just like this one. With you."

He didn't have to say it, but Camille knew they were both remembered the night of their senior year when they'd kissed behind a twinkling evergreen, reluctant to break apart and go home with their families. Life had been so different then, so full of possibilities. Her seventeen-year-old self would not have been able to imagine her twenty-six-year-old self standing in the same spot and purposely keeping Maddox at arm's length.

Even if she was tempted to let him come closer, tempted to feel his fingers entwined with hers. She pushed away that thought.

Being at peace with the past was one thing, but opening herself up to more hurt was another. Opening that door was reckless and stupid, and Camille was older and wiser now.

"Remember when I suggested a while ago that we could try starting over as friends," Maddox said.

"It's possible to be friendly," she said. "We're doing it right now." She kept her tone matter-of-fact, working hard to make sure the emotion and temptation she'd felt a moment earlier didn't show.

"And about starting over?" he asked.

She shook her head. "That implies that you think this would be going somewhere, as if it's the beginning of something. But it isn't."

Camille could tell her words stung Maddox, because he took a step back.

"We can be friendly just as we can be friendly to lots of other people on the island. And we should," she said practically. "The island isn't that big, and our businesses and families tend to overlap. But being friendly isn't the same as starting anything over."

He stood staring at her as if he'd almost won a game but then the rules had changed. After a moment, he glanced up at the festive hotel and then back at Camille.

"Well, then, happy Thanksgiving to an old friend," he said quietly, and then he turned and wound through the canopy of lights, disappearing from her view.

MADDOX ONLY AGREED to go back to the Winter Palace for hot cider after the Thanksgiving party because his son was clearly too wound up after seeing Santa to go to bed anytime soon. And it was only nine o'clock. They could hang out with Griffin and Rebecca for an hour or so and then he could persuade Ethan into a warm bath and flannel pajamas. Skipper would be okay for another hour before they needed to get home and let him outside.

Griffin had handed over their shared pickup truck at the end of the summer when Rebecca had finally brought her car to the island and agreed to stay on as their financial manager in addition to being the love of Griffin's life. Maddox pulled into the driveway at the Winter Palace, and he was surprised to see headlights behind him. He hadn't asked if Rebecca invited anyone else, but he now realized he and Ethan weren't the only guests.

"Santa said he'd see us in a month," Ethan said as they parked. "I was really glad, because I didn't know if he could come to an island."

"Of course he can," Maddox said. "He has a flying sleigh. Have you been worrying about that?"

"A little," Ethan admitted. "But it's okay now."

"If there are things bothering you, you should tell me. Okay? Promise me you'll ask if you have other big questions."

"Okay."

Maddox knew the next year would have its challenges as they all adjusted to Ethan's mom getting remarried and they tried out the new custody arrangement. The school year on the island, and the summer and weekends—weather permitting—with Ethan's mom. Maddox was getting the better end of the deal, with a lot more time than his ex-wife. Jennifer called Ethan frequently, and she'd already made requests for extra visits. She was a good mother, and Maddox wanted her to be happy.

His own happiness came entirely from his son and his island businesses.

"Hello," Camille said as soon as he opened the truck door. She had gotten out of the car behind him, which he recognized as Violet's. Jordan and Violet, longtime island friends, were already walking into the kitchen entrance of the Winter Palace, but Camille had paused by Maddox's truck. "I didn't know you were coming, too," she added.

"I hope you're not disappointed."

She laughed lightly. "We're all old friends, and since your brother is dating my best friend, this is just…part of life."

"A good part," Maddox said.

Ethan had managed his seat belt and opened his own door. He dashed into the ornate home, where he seemed almost as comfortable as he did at home with Maddox. The Winter Palace was theirs now, his and Griffin's, and his son would grow up enjoying parties and family meals there. Maddox could hardly believe how lucky he and his brother were and how quickly their lives had changed over the summer, going from scrambling for every dollar they put into their ferry and hotel to having enough money in the bank to fuel their dreams.

"I won't stay long," Camille said. "Rebecca and I are online shopping tomorrow, but I have to get in some work at the shop, too, so I'll have an early morning."

"I can only stay an hour before it'll be time to get Ethan home and let the dog out. I could give you a ride on our way."

Camille hesitated just long enough that he knew he was testing their tenuous friendship. She gave a little shrug. "We'll see, but thanks."

Maddox glanced toward the door his son had gone through. He knew Ethan was fine, and he wanted to continue the conversation he and Camille had started on the illuminated lawn at the Great Island Hotel. Was there really no future for them aside from polite friendship? What did he really want from her? Not having to endure the feeling that she hated him or harbored resentment had been freeing. But starting from where they were? Where would they go? His heart tugged him toward her, but he also had to consider his son. How would a relationship with Camille affect Ethan?

"We should get inside," Camille said. She took a step toward the door.

"Just one question first," Maddox said. "Why did you toss a marshmallow on my plate?"

Camille sighed. "It was impulsive, and I shouldn't have."

"Why did you?"

"I wanted… I thought it was a way to show myself that I could remember the past without letting it swamp me. I can think about fun things without dwelling on them."

"Or wanting to repeat them," Maddox said.

She nodded. "Definitely that."

"So I could say how nice it was growing up with you without there being any hidden land mines."

"You could," she said. "And I would say it was nice growing up with you and all the other people on the island. I tried walling off the past, but I think this is better. Focus on the good parts and move forward."

"So we're going to be friends again,"

Maddox said. "And if so, I need to know the rules."

"I haven't thought of all the rules."

"I have a few minutes. We could start a list."

"Okay," Camille said cautiously. "Maybe you could treat me like you do Violet or even one of my sisters. You grew up with them, too."

"True. Violet gave me a hug this evening when we greeted each other at the hotel, and I kissed her cheek."

He saw Camille swallow in the light radiating from the windows. Had he gone too far already?

"Violet is lovely, always has been," Camille said. "I keep waiting for her and Jordan to realize…"

"That they're perfect for each other?"

"Or something," Camille said. "But I don't think that was your point, was it? If we're going to be friends, we could withstand a friendly hug on a holiday. That's what you're saying, right?"

"Do you want to try?" he asked.

"If it gets me inside where there's warmth

and hot cider faster, then fine," she said. She held out her arms. "Friendly hug."

Maddox stepped toward her and slid his arms around her, pulling her close and hardly daring to breathe. Camille put her arms around him and gave his back a friendly pat. He closed his eyes and enjoyed the heaven of having Camille in his arms for three seconds, and then he released her and stepped back.

He was glad for the darkness and hoped his face didn't convey the lightning that had gone through him.

"That wasn't so bad, now was it?" she said. She sounded a bit breathless, but Maddox thought it might be that he was the one feeling off balance.

"We both survived," he said.

As they turned and walked into the house, he wondered how he was going to survive seeing Camille almost every day without wanting her in his arms, with her hair brushing his chin and her minty scent taking him straight back to the time when he had loved her desperately and then lost her.

When she'd come back to the island, his

goal had been to get to a place where he didn't feel he had to hide from her or keep apologizing. Now that they were beyond that place, maybe he should stop. Forgiveness was powerful, but it also had limits.

CHAPTER TWELVE

THE NUMBER OF Saturday morning shoppers was nothing like the crowds of the summer season, and Camille was glad. Thanksgiving was just past, and the island turned its attention to Christmas with childlike enthusiasm and mythological stamina. The Chamber of Commerce took care of putting wreaths on all the streetlights and stringing strands of white lights across the streets in a grid pattern. They began the weekend after Thanksgiving, and all the downtown shops joined in adding decorations steadily for the next few weeks.

Camille sat cross-legged in the front window of the Island Candy and Fudge shop, sorting out a strand of lights with a faulty bulb. Window displays downtown were imaginative, beautiful and competitive. She had to think of something great to adorn the huge front windows of the shop, and she hoped she'd be inspired by whatever she found in the storage room. Camille finished untangling the cords and outlining the windows in red and white lights. She watched them blink in candy-cane colors for a moment, and then she walked through the shop to the storage room in the back.

The storage room was sealed against mice and damp and usually housed huge bags of sugar and flour and bulk bags of fillings and candy flavorings. The storage room also had a wall of shelves in the back with holiday decorations, used mixers and bowls that were too good to throw away and paper records from nearly one hundred years of candy sales.

The island's theme for the year was Christmas Past, and Camille thought it was a perfect match for the upcoming bicentennial summer. She dusted off a box she found containing a model train and track, and then she rejected the idea. There had never been a train on the island, and she wanted her window to be an accurate historical representation of Christmas Island. She needed to set a good example if she was going to take a leading role in the bicentennial committee.

Camille took clear plastic coverings off a pair of elves in velvet costumes pulling taffy. It was cute and would be perfect for any other year, but this wasn't just any year. Would those elves work for the history theme? She shook her head and put them back on the shelf under their protective covers. *Maybe next year*, she thought, knowing that she would very likely be doing the shop windows for the rest of her life now that she had decided to take over her family's business.

This year, she had to get it right. What would tie the Christmas Past theme to the candy shop?

"Mom," Camille said as she dashed out of the storage room, "what do you think of a gingerbread house?"

Her mom looked up from a huge batch of fudge she was working on on a marble table. Melinda's cheeks were pink, and she breathed heavily from the exertion. Eating candy was easy, Camille thought, but making it was hard work.

"I love making little gingerbread houses. We haven't done that in a while."

"I'm thinking of a really big one," Camille said. She knew how much time it would take, but the idea was so perfect she couldn't resist. For all she knew, next year's theme would be holiday movies or winter sports. This was the perfect time for a gingerbread house representing a historic island building, and who better than a candy shop to make and display it?

"How big?"

"Something for the front window display that goes with the island history theme," Camille said. "What building on the island is the most iconic and would represent the past?"

"I think this one certainly does," her mother said.

Camille thought about it. "I love this place, and it does have a century of history, but it's a storefront, and its beauty may not come through in gingerbread. We need a really unique and interesting building."

"The church? Maybe the Great Island Hotel?"

"The hotel would be spectacular, but it's

already been done. Remember the huge model the pastry chefs did for the Christmas in July ball a few years ago? That was amazing, and I wouldn't even try to compete with it."

"Something else then," her mother said, expertly working the fudge into a long row that could be cut into slices as it formed and cooled.

"How about the Winter Palace?" Camille asked. "Can you imagine how perfect it would be as a gingerbread house with its porches and turrets? It will be like a Christmas castle."

Her mother sighed. "That is a perfect idea. But it's going to take time."

"Worth it?" Camille asked.

"Definitely. We'll start a batch of gingerbread sheets baking, and we'll start planning it while they bake. I just have to finish this batch of fudge first so it can get on the truck on Monday."

"I wish I'd thought of this a week ago," Camille said. She took the big paddle her mother was using on the fudge and began working it herself. "We could have made all the pieces already."

"It's only November 29," her mother said as she sipped a glass of water and sat down to watch Camille for a moment. "We have time. Especially if we call in a little help. You know how much your father loves to build things, and Cara has an artist's eye even if she claims she'd rather be in the barns."

"As soon as this fudge sets up, I'm going to dig out pictures of the Winter Palace to use as a guide," Camille said. "There must be some good ones in the town hall museum, or I can search back through online records."

"Don't you think it would be faster and easier to drive over there and take some pictures yourself?" her mother suggested. "You could get exactly the angles you want."

Camille smiled. "You're right. I'll go this morning while the light is good."

She finished the batch of fudge while her mother mixed gingerbread dough and pressed it into large sheets to bake. Even with their commercial ovens, it would take several hours to get enough sheets to work with, so Camille took advantage of the time and drove to the base of the driveway leading up to the Winter Palace. She had texted Rebecca in advance to ask permission just in case Rebecca or Griffin noticed and wondered. Camille knew her friend would probably be in the home's library, where she had set up a business office for May Ferry Line.

Griffin was probably not home. He and Maddox were spending their winter months supervising and working on the construction of their new dock and ticket office, because they were doubling the size of their operation. With an island hotel to run and a major expansion of his ferry line, not to mention custody of his son for most of the year, Camille knew Maddox had plenty to keep his time occupied.

And so did she. As busy as they both were, it should be very easy to keep their friendship in perspective.

Camille parked and got out, considering her angles. The sky was bright blue with a winter sun, and the trees surrounding the magnificent home were bare. A few evergreens filled out the landscaping around the home without detracting from its architectural lines. Light snow lay in patches on the roof, and someone had hung wreaths from all the windows and garlands along the porch railings, making it already look a bit like a gingerbread house. It was a perfect opportunity to capture the lines and angles of the house so she could recreate the entire thing out of sugar.

She heard a vehicle stop on the road right behind her as she held up her smartphone and took pictures.

"If you'd like a close-up, I know the owners," she heard Maddox's voice say.

Camille turned with a smile, ready to share her plans with Maddox, but she stopped and her breath caught. Maddox was in the driver's seat of his pickup with Ethan in the middle and his ex-wife in the passenger seat. The whole family, as if they were on a sightseeing trip around the island. The warmth that had started to melt the hard ice between her and Maddox turned cold as Camille looked at the face of the woman Maddox had chosen over her on that long-ago weekend that had changed their lives.

IT WOULD HAVE been easier and wiser to just drive past Camille's car. But as soon as he saw her silhouette with her cell phone raised toward the home on the hill, curiosity got the better of him.

He pulled off the road and rolled down his window despite the cold temperatures.

"I've heard the owners are thinking of selling it off and moving to New York City," Camille said.

Her tone was light, but Maddox couldn't miss the glance she cast over at his passenger. There was no doubt she knew who Jennifer was.

"They do have ferry boats there," Maddox said. "Why are you taking pictures of the place? Are you pretending to be a tourist for the day?"

"Gingerbread house," Camille said. She waved to Ethan and Jennifer, acknowledging them even though Maddox knew she couldn't be happy about the memories they would dredge up. "The downtown decorating theme is Christmas Past," she said. Her eyes flickered toward Jennifer and then back to him. "And what better idea for a candy shop than to have a gingerbread house in the window representing a historic island building?"

"Can we eat it?" Ethan asked.

Camille smiled at the boy. "Gingerbread houses aren't the best for eating," she said. "And it's going to be on display for weeks, so it won't taste very fresh. I could offer you gingerbread cookies instead the next time you come in my shop."

"Okay," the boy said. "But I want to see the house."

"I'll let you know when it's done," she said. "It's going to be a big challenge, and I hope it will turn out."

"I'm sure it will," Jennifer said. "You're a candy expert, right?"

Maddox was glad his ex-wife hadn't called Camille a candy girl, because he vividly remembered how she'd hated that. Being a candy expert was a compliment, but he still thought he would be wise to drive away as quickly as he could.

"Are you staying long?" Camille asked. "I don't know if it will be done before you…leave."

"Just for the day," Jennifer said. "I flew in because Ethan wanted to show me his new room, and Maddox and I had some business. But I'm leaving on a plane later today."

Camille nodded. "There are storms coming later, so—"

"That's what Maddox said, but I'll be fine. I'll leave in plenty of time so I don't get stuck out here."

Camille's face showed a hint of annoyance, and Maddox didn't blame her. His ex had cut off Camille's sentence but also implied that being on Christmas Island was an inconvenience.

Camille turned back to him. "I hope you don't mind if I use your family's home as my inspiration."

"Not at all. It's on the island souvenir calendar every year, and I'm sure Aunt Flora will be delighted to see pictures of her house as a gingerbread creation."

"You'll have to tell her all about it when you see her for Christmas," Camille said.

"You're spending Christmas with her?" Jennifer asked. "I thought you were going to be here."

"We are. I'm going to pick her up when I pick up Ethan from your wedding."

"I didn't know that," Jennifer said.

"I didn't think you would care. You'll be on your honeymoon in Europe."

He noticed that Camille took a step back, as if she didn't want anything to do with a tense conversation between Maddox and his ex-wife, and he couldn't blame her. He gave Camille a little wave. "Good luck with your project."

"Thanks," she said. She went back to taking photos, and Maddox rolled up his window and put the truck in gear.

"She hasn't changed much," Jennifer said.

"You know the candy lady?" Ethan asked.

"I've met her before," Jennifer said. "It's not a big island, so it's not hard to meet everybody who lives here. Plus, my family used to come to the island and visit every year. So, she's back working at the family candy store? I thought she moved away."

"She did, but she came home," Maddox said. He liked the way the word *home* sounded. Jennifer would never consider the island home, would never understand what it meant for him to live and raise his son here. "Ethan will have to show you all the improvements we've made to the house recently. I know it's been a few years since you've been out to the island, so you'll notice quite a few things are different now that my parents are gone and Griffin has moved out."

"We have a swing set and a slide in the backyard," Ethan said. "And we're making a game room in the basement."

"That sounds wonderful," Jennifer said. "Our new house in Lakeside is going to have a pool, and since you'll be spending summers with me, you can swim all day and invite your friends."

"Can we get a pool, too, Dad?"

Maddox glanced at his son and shook his head. "We live on an island. We don't need a pool."

"Okay," Ethan agreed.

Maddox turned into the driveway of the ranch house where he'd grown up. It wasn't huge, but it had a sunset view every day of the year, plenty of yard and trees, and years of happy memories. His father had inherited the place along with the ferry line, and Maddox hoped the boy next to him would do the same. The house had cedar siding and a long front porch perfect for watching sunsets. The one-story structure wasn't imaginative or fancy, but it was cozy and solid. The home had weathered a century of island winters.

"You should have taken the Winter Palace instead of letting your brother have it," Jennifer commented as Maddox parked.

"I asked for this place instead," Maddox said, tamping down a flare of irritation. "I grew up here, and there's plenty of room for me and Ethan. Great place to be a kid."

"I just want what's best for him," she said.

"We both do," Maddox said.

He got out of the truck, anxious to escape its confines before something was said that Ethan would have questions about later. The boy heard everything even when he didn't seem to be paying attention.

"Come see the tire swing," Ethan told his mother.

"It's cold," she protested.

"We'll go fast," he said.

Maddox smiled as his son dragged Jennifer around the attached garage to the backyard, where a tire swing hung from a magnificent oak tree. Maddox had replaced the rope and the tire, but the swing was in the same location as the one he and his brother had played on, dared each other to jump off and dangled their feet from as children. He wished that Ethan had a sibling, but he vowed to be a friend and playmate to the boy. And there were other children his age on the island to grow up with, just as he and Griffin had made lifelong friends. With people like Camille.

A stiff breeze buffeted Maddox as he let Skipper into the yard and then walked around the garage to watch his son demonstrate the tire swing. He glanced up and saw that, already, some dark clouds were moving in from the west. He needed to review the paperwork his ex-wife had brought over, show her that he was providing an excellent and safe home, and then get her to the island airport before she ended up staying the night.

CHAPTER THIRTEEN

CAMILLE STUDIED THE photographs of the
Winter Palace she'd printed on the color
printer in the back of the store. Using the
pictures as a guide, she sketched pencil
outlines on parchment paper spread on the
large marble fudge tables. The scale was
the hard part. The Victorian home had one
large and one small turret, three stories of
living space, an upper and lower balcony,
and a lower level built into the hillside.
She wanted to replicate it as closely as she
could so it would be instantly recognizable.

The architectural details were the necessary but less creative part of the job. When
it came time to fill parchment bags with
white, red and green royal icing to pipe in
all the details, the fun would really start.
She couldn't wait to make the fish scales on
the roof and add the ornate wooden decorative elements and the pillars and chimneys.

She would decorate the home for Christmas using icing, and there would be colored bulbs, wreaths and garlands. Little bits of candy cane and gumdrops would add color and texture. Camille knew her project was ambitious, and she hoped she would produce a shop window that would wow all of Christmas Island.

Her father came through the back door of the candy store with a wood platform in his hands and some long wood rods tucked under one arm.

"This is the base, and I want to use dowel rods as internal pillars to give it some structure. I have as much faith in the staying power of royal icing as the next guy, but this is going to be a big gingerbread house, and we don't want the roof caving in or the walls collapsing."

"Thanks," Camille said. "Should we assemble it here or in the window, where it's going to go?"

"That depends if you want it to be a surprise or not. There's no way we'll get it all done tonight—at least, I really doubt it— so people will see that it's a work in progress if we assemble it in the window. Even though that's also the safest bet so we won't have to move it once it's done."

"I'm okay with people seeing the work in progress," Camille said. "I'm a work in progress, too."

Ron Peterson laughed. "You're perfect just as you are. Look at you, reinventing our shop, going online, shipping all over the country. You're doing things I would have been afraid to do."

"You aren't afraid of change," Camille said.

"Then why didn't I do it?" he asked.

"You…didn't want to?"

Her dad leaned both elbows on the marble table. "I did make some changes when I took over from my parents." He smiled. "I wanted to put my own stamp on the shop, which I think you can understand."

Camille nodded and smiled back. "What changes did you make?"

"Nothing as bold as you, but I did upgrade to commercial ovens and mixers so we could up our volume. And I added staff to keep up with increased demand. Only a few people, but it made a difference. Still, our business has been basically the same for almost a hundred years."

"And it was working well," Camille said.

"If you call flat sales and a loyal but basically static customer base working well, then yes," he said. "But you brought something back to the island that was missing. Determination and bravery. I'm proud of you."

Camille wondered if her father would be proud of her if he knew how often she doubted herself, and if he knew she'd only decided to come back to Christmas Island when she found out her sister Chloe was leaving. She hadn't wanted to compete with her for the title of most important daughter. And she hadn't been ready to come back and face her past with Maddox, either. Did he really think she was brave, or did he suspect the truth—her desperation to prove herself?

"You'll have to wait and see how this all turns out before you nominate me for candy girl of the year," she said.

Her phone pinged with a text message, and she saw Violet's name on the screen. It was dark outside with heavy rain and wind, but inside the candy shop it was warm, light and fragrant with gingerbread. Across the street, the lights were also on in Violet's Island Boutique, and Camille imagined her friend was either stocking or cleaning or possibly working up a design for her storefront windows, too.

Can I come over? Violet texted. Chocolate emergency.

Camille sent her a heart and smiley face emoji. Her friend rushed through the front door and closed it firmly behind her just one minute later.

"Yowza, the weather," Violet said. "I may stay the whole night in my store so I don't have to drive home in this storm."

"We're staying late working on our window display, and you're welcome to stick around until you get tired of eating chocolate and smelling gingerbread."

"That will never happen," Violet said. She approached the marble table and looked at the photographs and sketches. "That's the Winter Palace? Are you planning to invade it and search for hidden passageways?" Violet pointed out the sketches and attempts at scale drawings on the white paper. "I've always thought that a house as old and fabulous as that one must have some wonderful secrets."

"I think the owner did, considering her surprise decision to leave the home and her fortune to Griffin and Maddox May," Camille said.

Violet sighed. "That was so romantic, the story of Flora Winter's long-lost love being their grandfather. I can't imagine pining away for someone for decades like that."

Camille wanted to mention that their circle of friends had invested some time in wondering if Violet and Jordan were ever going to recognize the force of attraction between them. However, she chose to steer clear of any talk of romance, especially because her father was in the room, and also because of the association with Maddox May.

She had enough to do.

"Gingerbread house," she said, switching the subject back to the drawings. "It's going in the front window as our display to go along with the history theme this year."

"Christmas Past," Violet said. "I'm in love with that theme, and I think we should do it every year. Do you have any pull with the Chamber of Commerce? Do you think you could persuade them to keep the same theme for the rest of my life?"

"Why?" Camille asked, laughing.

"Because old-fashioned dresses and clothing are the very best. I was actually making a gown for the front window. Red velvet with a capelet trimmed in white fur. Faux fur, of course," she added. "It will look perfect for a romantic sleigh ride at the turn of the last century." She sighed. "I wish people still dressed like that."

Camille's father's phone sounded an alarm, and he ran over to the coatrack and dug the phone from his jacket pocket. There was a small but dedicated volunteer firefighter and first responder force on the island, and Camille's dad had been part of it her entire life. She remembered him dashing out in the middle of the night or leaving a batch of fudge half-stirred at the shop when someone was in need.

"Boat sinking offshore," he said. "Heaven help them in this storm."

"What can you do?" Camille said.

"Nothing without a sturdy boat, and the coast guard is forty minutes away," he said, reading off his phone. "I'm going down to the harbor to see if there are any boats still in the water that we could take out, but it'll be risky."

"I'll come, too," Camille said. She glanced out the front window and saw Maddox's pickup truck speed past. "The ferry," she said. "Is it heavy-duty enough?"

Her father shook his head grimly as he zipped his jacket and pulled on a hat. "Maybe, but it's risky."

She didn't want her dad to risk his life on the wild lake, but would Maddox or Griffin? Camille and Violet tossed on their winter coats and hats and followed Camille's dad as they ran down the street. What had begun as heavy rain had turned to ice while Camille and her father worked on the gingerbread display. The streets were slippery, and ice clung to streetlights and railings.

"This is bad," Violet said.

They reached the docks downtown and found several vehicles and almost a dozen other people in the shelter of the ticket office.

"Can you see the boat?" Griffin asked as he joined the group.

Maddox pointed toward a moving light out on the lake in the opposite direction of the mainland. "That's got to be it. Why anyone is out there on a night like this, I have no idea."

Griffin swiped rainwater and snowflakes from his forehead. "And the coast guard?"

Camille's dad shook his head. "My message said they're tied up, can't get here for thirty minutes."

"Those poor souls on that boat don't have thirty minutes," Luke Byrnes said. Camille recognized the man as the new maintenance man at the Great Island Hotel. "I was in the navy, did some rescue training. I'll go along if anyone's got a solid boat."

"I've got a boat," Maddox said. "But I don't want too many people risking their lives."

"We'll go," Griffin said. "Me and Maddox."

"You've got a family, too," Camille's dad said to Maddox.

"Ethan's not alone. My ex is with him at my house. Couldn't fly back because of the weather. I'm not sending my brother out alone on the ferry."

Camille wanted to say something, but she couldn't speak past the lump in her throat. And she didn't know what she would have said anyway. Would she urge them not to go and try to save whoever was on that sinking boat? Would she tell them to be careful—advice they almost certainly didn't need?

"I'll join you," Camille's father said.

That jolted her and gave her back the power of speech. She grabbed his arm. "You will not," she said.

"No choice," he said. He lowered his voice. "I'll come back. We've got a big project going on, and I want to see how it turns out."

Camille didn't know if he meant the gingerbread house or the family business. Either way, she didn't want him to go out on the wild dark lake, but he was already walking to the ferry with Griffin and Maddox. Luke Byrnes stayed with the crowd assembled onshore, and they all watched as Griffin went up in the pilothouse and started the engines. Maddox and Camille's dad threw off the shorelines and pulled on life preservers.

The ferry pitched and surged as it began moving, the waves battering it even though it was barely away from the dock. How much worse would it be as they got out on the open lake and made their way to the foundering boat? Violet put her arm around Camille. "Should we call the rest of your family?"

"No," Camille said. "They'll panic."

"You're not panicking."

"Yes, I am. You just can't see it."

Violet put a hand over her mouth as she watched the ferry lights dim in the stormy night. "We just have to have faith in Griffin and Maddox. I know they've been out before in horrible weather. They've grown up on this lake. If anyone can save those boaters and come back in one piece, it's the May brothers."

"I hope so," Camille said. Her voice was choked with emotion. Her father was bravely risking his own skin to help someone, and she wasn't surprised. He was the kind of man who never looked away when anyone needed a hand. Griffin and Maddox…they had so much to live for, just like her dad. They had a new inheritance. Griffin had finally found true love with Rebecca. Maddox had his son and a chance to give the boy the idyllic childhood they'd all enjoyed on Christmas Island.

Her heart was in physical pain as the ferry lights disappeared in the night, and she felt Rebecca slide an arm around her from the other side.

"I'm breaking up with Griffin as soon as he gets back. I can't handle this," Rebecca said through tears.

Camille laughed for one second, breaking loose some of the terrible tension as they watched, powerless, from the shore.

MADDOX SHIVERED INSIDE his heavy waterproof coat. He knew that if he ended up in the lake, he'd have to shed that coat immediately so it wouldn't pull him under. No matter how good a swimmer he was, no one was a match for the darkness, the cold and the waves. Spray came off the front of the ferry as his brother piloted it toward the sinking boat, and the shocking cold reminded him of the stakes.

"How close do you think we can get?"

Ron Peterson yelled over the wind. "Can we throw lines or life rings?"

"I hope so." Maddox couldn't think of another way of getting the sinking boat's passengers onto the ferry. He just hoped they weren't already too late.

Griffin flipped on the powerful overhead lights on the ferry and illuminated the water ahead of them. They were almost within range of the vessel in trouble. Maddox swiped water from his face. Although the ferry was heavy and sat low in the water, it wasn't built for cutting through heavy waves. Water rolled over the deck, and he and Camille's dad held on to the cold steel of the front railing.

The lights on the sinking boat suddenly went out, and Maddox's heart stopped for a minute. Had the entire boat slipped under the water? If so, the chance of finding any survivors floating in the lake was slim.

"Do you see it at all?" Ron yelled. "I lost it."

Maddox scanned the darkness, hoping for any sign of the boat. "There," he yelled. He pointed, knowing his brother would be able to see him in the ferry's lights even if

Griffin couldn't see the endangered boat. Maddox felt the ferry turn slightly and knew his brother was following his lead. He just hoped he was right about the dark shape. If it wasn't the boat, people could die.

A moment later, he felt Camille's dad slap him on the back. "That's it. Right there."

Maddox saw it at the same time. The thirty-foot powerboat was on its side but still above water, and in the powerful lights from the ferry, Maddox saw two people clinging to the gunwales.

They were barely in time. Maddox waved at Griffin. He felt the engines gear down as the ferry slowed and came as close to the sinking boat as they could get without crashing into it. Maddox looped a rope around Camille's dad and tied it off to the railing. "Just in case," he said. "I don't want you getting washed overboard as we try this."

"What about you?"

Maddox snapped a rope to his life jacket, and Camille's dad nodded.

"Hey," Maddox yelled to the people on the wrecked boat, hoping they could hear him over the ferry's engine and the roaring wind and waves. "I'm going to throw you a line."

Griffin adjusted the searchlights, and they could see the two people on the sinking boat clearly now. They both wore orange life preservers.

"Thank God," Camille's dad said.

"We just have to get them over here," Maddox said. He held a coil of rope with a float attached to the end. Camille's dad steadied him with a hand on his back as he threw it to one of the men. The man reached for it, lost his balance and slipped into the water. His friend grabbed for his life jacket and pulled him back up. The boat slipped lower and rolled farther off center.

"Almost out of chances," Maddox muttered. If they didn't catch it this time, the chances of rescue were dimming.

"You've got this," Ron said.

Maddox threw the rope again and held his breath while the float sailed in an arc and sank down right next to the men. "Get it," he said, willing them to grab the line this time. One of the men reached for the rope, dipped under the water and then emerged with the float in his hands. He reached out for his friend, and they both grabbed the rope.

"Pulling you in," Maddox yelled. He braced his feet on the inside of the ferry's front railing, and Camille's dad did the same. Together, they pulled hand over hand as the survivors inched toward the ferry. The waves battered the men and slowed them, and Maddox used all his strength to fight the lake. The ferry continued to pitch and bob, and Maddox felt sweat running under his clothes while freezing lake water soaked him from the outside.

Ron Peterson was thirty years older than he was, but the man pulled like a machine, adrenaline fueling his efforts. Maddox wished his brother could come and help them, but if Griffin didn't hold the ferry steady, they'd all be in trouble.

The men were halfway to the ferry when a huge wave hit the boat. Ron lost his balance, and his feet washed out from under him. The water rushed him toward the car entrance, where the railing wasn't solid and there was a space large enough for a person to slip through. His feet were already under the railing before Maddox could reach him. He looped the rope around a bulkhead and kept hold of it while he skidded over to Ron and grabbed the back of his jacket. The older man scrambled to his knees and pulled himself to his feet.

"Thanks," Ron said as he struggled a moment to catch his breath. "Thought I was going overboard."

They went back to pulling in the swimmers and tugged them the rest of the way toward the boat. Ron held tension on the rope so they couldn't slip away, and Maddox leaned through the car entrance opening that had nearly claimed Ron as he pulled the rescued men on board one at a time.

Camille's dad stayed inside the pilothouse with the two rescued men, trying to warm them up, and Maddox stood alone on the deck of the ferry as it approached the dock. He threw a line ashore, and several people, including one of their regular dockhands, were there to grab it.

When they returned to the dock, Maddox saw dozens of people waiting onshore.

Neither of the rescued boaters needed medical care other than to warm up as quickly as possible. Bystanders offered blankets to the shivering men. Maddox and Griffin had already agreed to put them up in empty rooms at their hotel for the night until it was safe for them to leave the island. The coast guard had radioed that they could make a pickup at the island airport if the men were injured, but both men declined, grateful that their late-season fishing trip hadn't ended with their deaths.

"You should have waited for me, boss, I would have gone with you," a dockhand said.

Maddox shook his head. "I wouldn't have risked your life."

Camille, Rebecca and Violet stood huddled in the overhang of the ticket building, but they rushed toward the boat as soon as it was secured. The five men on the ferry left together. Camille's mother waited with her van running, lights on. She ran toward them, gave her husband a bear hug and then shooed the other two men into her van, telling them not to worry about being wet.

"Griffin called," Camille said. "Mom's

taking them to the hotel, and Hadley is already there making sure their rooms are ready."

"Thanks," Maddox said. He glanced around, wondering if Ethan and Jennifer were in the crowd, but he didn't see them. It was just as well. He didn't want his son out in the weather and worrying about his dad. Jennifer had made the right choice staying home.

Suddenly, Camille threw her arms around him and held him close. He was frozen from the rain, snow and wind, but he didn't care. Having her in his arms warmed him all the way through. It made every terrifying moment on the boat and the ache in his arms and muscles worthwhile.

"Come back to the candy store," Ron said. "I owe you some coffee for saving my life, and we all need to warm up."

Maddox felt Camille jerk back. She put an arm out for her dad while still keeping one around Maddox. "Saving your life?"

Her dad smiled. "It's okay. I almost went in the drink, but Maddox grabbed me and hauled me in like a big fish."

Camille hugged them both at the same time. "We're not telling Mom," she said.

"Works for me. I'm sure she'll come to the shop as soon as she drops the fishermen off at the hotel. I'll tell her it was no big deal, and Maddox will back me up."

Camille laughed. "She won't believe it, but you can try."

By the time they got to the candy shop, Cara and Chloe were already waiting with bath towels, dry clothing, coffee and a hot tray of freshly baked sweet bread.

"Griffin and Rebecca are coming, too," Camille told Maddox as she took his wet coat and hung it by the front door. "Griffin wanted to run home and change first."

"I should call home," he said. He didn't want to say Jennifer's name, but he needed to let her know he was safe and would be coming back later. It was common courtesy, and he wanted her to put Ethan to bed knowing his dad would be there when he woke up the next day.

"Of course," Camille said, her glance steady. "Go ahead and use the back room, and I'll pour you some coffee in the meantime."

Maddox went in the back of the store, called his ex-wife and gave her a brief explanation, and then asked her to put Ethan on the line. He knew the boy would still be awake, even though it was past his bedtime. He told his son about the rescue and promised to give him all the details the next day if he went to bed and tried to go to sleep.

He was smiling when he went back into the candy store and took a cup of coffee from Camille. Melinda was there fussing over Ron, and Camille's sisters were making sure everyone had fresh icing on their sweet bread. Despite the tension and danger of the storm, life on Christmas Island was a slice of heaven, and Maddox knew it was due to the people who lived there.

"Thank you," he said. "I tried to persuade Ethan to go to bed, but I don't know if I was successful. I shouldn't stay too long."

"I just want you to dry off and get something warm in your stomach before you go out again."

"And get cold and wet all over again," he said.

"I wish—"

"It's okay. I'll survive. We're islanders, right?"

Maddox imagined for a moment that Camille would invite him over. Her apartment was upstairs and one building over, but Maddox knew it was possible to get there without going outside. A back hallway connected most of the downtown buildings, making the long winters more bearable for residents. He wasn't actually angling for an invitation to her apartment for the night—that would be out of the question, and he needed to get home—but he was glad Camille would stay dry. She'd stood in the storm waiting for the ferry to return, and she had to be nearly as cold and wet as he was.

"Wet islanders," she said with a smile that made him forget his damp shirt clinging to his torso. "Come see my plans for the gingerbread house replica of your family's mansion."

Camille showed him her photographs and patterns. Large sheets of baked gingerbread sat waiting on the wide countertops and fudge tables.

"Will you be up till dawn working on this?" he asked.

"I was planning to, but I think we've all had enough excitement for one night."

The police chief came in a few minutes later and got Maddox's help with the report. He'd already visited the two marooned fishermen and reported that they seemed comfortable and in good spirits. They were using the hotel phone to call their families, because their cell phones had been lost in the lake. Maddox and Griffin supplied details for the official report, and Maddox reluctantly finished his coffee and rolls and pulled on his wet coat.

"Thank you," Camille said. "For making sure everyone came back safely."

"Thank you for waiting in the rain and giving us a warm welcome."

"Maddox," she said quickly, as if she was afraid to stall over his name. "Let me buy you dinner one of these days. To say thank you for keeping my dad safe." She smiled. "He's getting too old to do those things, even though he wouldn't agree with me."

They stood just inside the doorway, and Camille glanced over her shoulder. Was she wondering what people would think if they saw the two of them talking? What would people say if they saw them out having dinner together?

"I can ask Dorothy to babysit. She has yarn club one night and book club another one, but I'll ask her for her first available slot."

Camille nodded. "Text me. And I'm buying."

"Even if we go to my hotel's restaurant? It's our best option for good food this time of year."

"Yes," she said with a smile.

For a moment, Maddox thought about what would have happened if he hadn't screwed up seven years earlier. Camille might be his wife now. They'd go home together and talk about the night's events. Instead, he dodged the rain and snow on the way to his truck to make the drive around the island to his house, where he hoped his ex-wife had left at least one light on for him.

CHAPTER FOURTEEN

It had been her idea, Camille reminded herself three nights later as she agonized over what to wear for her dinner with Maddox. It was a friendly thank-you dinner, but it felt more like the top step of a very steep staircase. She should have been satisfied with a hug and a thank-you instead of letting the emotions of the evening lead her into territory she wasn't equipped to handle. Camille had boiled and rolled hundreds of pounds of fudge as she considered her own reaction to seeing Maddox walk off the ferry that stormy night.

"Don't read into it," she said aloud as she selected a navy blue sweater and gray pants for her dinner with Maddox. The hotel bar was upscale casual, and the boatneck sweater with a silver necklace would be perfect. She had grown up wearing candy colors, but she felt beautiful in deep jewel tones as an adult.

Did she want to look beautiful for Maddox? She shook her head. She wanted to feel beautiful for herself. She pulled on her long red wool coat, stepped into her black ankle boots and took the back stairs from her place. She'd agreed to meet him at the restaurant, because it was more of a "just friends" thing to do.

Maddox leaned an elbow on the reception desk of the empty hotel lobby.

"Full house tonight?" Camille asked.

He laughed and shook his head. "Very seldom in the winter. There's the festival coming up, of course, and then the week of Christmas we'll fill all the rooms because of your sister's wedding, but we make our money when the ferry's running."

"Sounds like a piece of cake," she said playfully.

"When the weather's good."

Camille sobered. "Which is why we're here. Thank you again for not letting my dad make my mom a widow with his well-intentioned heroism."

"Is that the only reason we're here?" Maddox asked.

Camille pulled off her black leather gloves one finger at a time, buying her a moment to construct an answer. "I'd also like to eat," she said. "I've worked hard all day making Christmas candy and boxing it to ship, but I didn't even steal any for myself."

Maddox held out an arm. "I have a table reserved."

Camille put her hand lightly on his arm, but she didn't allow any other parts of their bodies to touch as they walked to a table behind the piano, where the bar was quiet. Was he hoping for intimate conversation or just respecting her privacy?

Maddox took off his coat and held out a hand, offering to take hers. She regarded him as he went to hang them up. He wore a blue-and-white-striped oxford and black pants. He looked like a man, not the boy she remembered. His dark hair was still cut very short, and his lake-blue eyes hadn't changed, but there were a few wrinkles around them. There was no doubt he'd grown up a lot since she'd left…but had he really changed at all?

"Did you tell Ethan you were having dinner with the candy lady tonight?" she asked as they sat.

Maddox smiled. "I told him I was having dinner with a friend."

That was probably best. She didn't want Maddox to have to explain anything about their relationship, past or present, to his son. There was no need. To Ethan, she was just another of his dad's friends from the island.

"If I'd told Ethan my dinner date was you, I'd have to bring home treats, and Dorothy already told me she was going to bake Christmas cookies with him tonight."

"You can never have too many sweets," Camille said.

"With a six-year-old, yes, you can."

Camille laughed. "Have you tried baking Christmas cookies with him, too?"

Maddox shook his head. "Not one of my skills."

"Anyone can learn."

"I'll let Dorothy spoil him. She misses her grandchildren, and Ethan fills that hole for her."

Camille wanted to ask if Ethan missed his grandmothers, but she knew Maddox and Griffin's mom had moved to Texas with her sister, and she didn't know anything about Jennifer's family. Maybe Ethan had a very doting grandmother on his mother's side who was sad that he'd spend more than half the year away from her on the island.

Living on Christmas Island, or any island, was a choice that came with consequences for the island residents and their relatives and friends on the mainland. Camille knew firsthand that it was hard to be away, and she'd only made that decision for seven years because she believed it was best for her.

With each day back on the island, with the challenges and excitement of running her family's company, she was more convinced she'd made the right choice.

"I haven't baked cookies with Ethan, but we did walk back into the woods and choose our tree. We'll go back and cut it down next week and set it up in the living room. Are you having a tree in your apartment this year?"

Camille cocked her head. "I hadn't thought about it. I've been so busy decorating the shop windows and filling our online Christmas orders that you'd never even know it's Christmas by looking at my apartment."

"Unless you looked outside at the street," Maddox said.

"I have to close my curtains to be able to sleep. The lights are beautiful on the street, but they're bright."

"I've always liked that," Maddox said. "I missed Christmas here for the two years when I lived…on the mainland, and it wasn't the same."

Camille smiled. "I know what you mean. Chicago had its own amazing holiday traditions, but it's not Christmas Island."

Their eyes met, and the tug of the past and all they had shared was so strong that Camille scooted her chair back and looked away. She hadn't come to dinner to rekindle those feelings. Her plan for dealing with the past—specifically Maddox—was to acknowledge it just to the point where it didn't have any control over her. As a person would flip on a light in a dark room to prove there was nothing in there to fear, that's how she was handling the complex emotions of the past. There was nothing hidden in the corners. It had all been exposed.

"We have a limited menu in the winter," Maddox said. "I hope you'll find something you like."

Camille took the menu he held out, and she was glad to have something to think about other than the way one long look in a dimly lit piano bar could unnerve her. She wouldn't be undone by a look from someone who had broken her heart too long ago to matter.

MADDOX RESOLVED TO stick to safe topics as he handed over a menu. When you got your foot caught in quicksand, the best thing to do was freeze. Only very slow movements would prevent him from getting sucked down in the quicksand of his relationship with Camille. He had too many other demands on his heart and his time to do what his brother thought he was trying to do—win Camille back.

There was no winning in a game he'd cheated in once. He doubted Camille would even play.

"I was thinking of talking with you about

a little business matter," he said. "And before you ask, Rebecca already knows about this and has approved it."

"I wasn't going to ask that. I'm sure you have some great plans of your own."

Maddox laughed. "My brother is very lucky that we have someone who understands business, or we'd be panicked even looking at our bank account. I'm grateful to Aunt Flora for her confidence in us—"

"It was her love for you that made her leave you millions," Camille said. "Confidence is a different matter entirely."

"I can't argue with that. So, I'm grateful for her love but even more grateful that my brother fell in love with a business genius at the same time."

"Rebecca is lucky, too," Camille said. "She didn't grow up like us, as I'm sure you know. I can't imagine bouncing from one foster home to the next. Somehow, it made her stronger, and she's the most loyal and generous person I know. I've run some of my business ideas past her, too. Not that she was surprised. When we were college roommates, she helped me with any econ or accounting classes I took."

"Not history?"

"I didn't need any help with that. I love digging around in the past because it's the best way—"

Maddox noticed a flush on Camille's cheeks as she looked back down at her menu.

"What were you going to say?" he asked.

"I was going to say that it's the best way to ensure you don't make the same mistakes that have been made in the past," she said quietly, not meeting his eyes.

"But people still do, don't they?"

Camille slowly raised her eyes to his. "Tragically, yes."

Hadley came over. "It's a small menu, so I'd bet you two have had time to decide," she said.

Maddox had already known what he wanted before the night started. The winter pot roast was his favorite, and it tasted like home cooking. Being a single dad had tapped out his cooking skills, but he planned to try some new kitchen attempts after the holiday. He couldn't let his son grow up on mac and cheese from a box.

"I was thinking of the winter pot roast,"

Camille said. "With dinner rolls and a house salad."

"Same," Maddox said.

"You always have that," Hadley said as she rolled her eyes at him and turned toward the kitchen.

"Do you always have that?" Camille asked.

"If *always* means a few times a week for the past few months, then yes. I usually get it to take home, though, so it's a nice treat to enjoy it hot right here in the restaurant."

"So, what's the business idea you wanted to talk about?"

"Our dock over in Lakeside. Here on the island, it's pretty simple. People ride or bike up, and they just get on the boat and that's it. But over on the mainland, they arrive early, linger a bit, sometimes wait for the ferry, make sure they're early to get their cars parked, that kind of stuff."

"Okay," Camille said. "So you want to entertain them?"

"Not so much entertain. We want to build an actual passenger terminal, indoors, with seating and something interesting to look at while they wait for their

ferry. So, maybe a snack bar or gift shop—
that's easy enough—but I want something
with some substance."

"Maybe a display of historic photographs
of the island?" Camille asked. "Framed and
with plaques next to them giving details
and information about Christmas Island
and its heritage?"

"Exactly. Do you think that's doable?"

"If you know what you're doing, yes,"
Camille said.

"That's why I need you. I was kicking
something like this around, but then after
the Thanksgiving event at the hotel, I realized you were really getting involved in
island history and you might be able to put
together the pictures."

"Curate a collection," Camille said.

"See, you even know what to call it.
You're perfect for this."

Camille tilted her head. "Perfect, except
for the fact that I've already gotten volunteered to work on the official bicentennial
for the island, including, perhaps, an actual book. Plus, you may have noticed I'm
building a candy empire that I hope will
stretch across the continent."

"So, next week maybe?" he asked.

Camille laughed. "Next year, if we're lucky."

He smiled. "You'll consider helping us? It would be such a nice gateway to the island, and I could promise to direct all tourists to your fudge shop as soon as they get off the boat."

"I'll think about it after the holidays and my sister's wedding. After I ship all the candy and send Chloe off on her honeymoon, I might even have time to finish unpacking my stuff."

"Thank you," Maddox said. "We really want to get this ferry expansion right. If we just add another boat, it's more of the same. We need to offer an experience if we want to grow our business meaningfully."

"You have this hotel."

He nodded. "It would be easy to be satisfied with that, but I think you know what it feels like to want something more."

"No doubt. I believe the candy shop can be so much more."

Maddox tipped his glass against hers and clinked it. "A toast to wanting more."

Maddox was relieved that Hadley showed

up with salads and rolls so he didn't have to think about other things he wanted but was unlikely to get, no matter how much hard work he put in.

After dinner, they put on their coats and walked to the door. Maddox was sure Camille was going to say good-night and make the short walk home. Both sides of the street had a row of shop fronts with two stories above them containing either storage or housing. A few hotels broke the downtown pattern, the Holiday Hotel owned by himself and his brother being one of them.

"I have something I want you to see," Camille said.

"Where are we going?"

"To the fabulous Winter Palace for a Christmas holiday," she said. "We just finished it late this afternoon, and I can't wait to see it all lit up."

They crossed the street and walked one block, pausing under the familiar striped awnings of her family's store. In the window, Maddox saw a replica of Flora Winter's stunning island mansion. It was recreated in gingerbread and colorful icing, but anyone would recognize the home with its turrets and porches.

"I can't believe it," he said.

"Do you think it looks like the real thing?"

"Even better. It's like a fantasy version. Exactly what you'd expect, but with enough unexpected twists and touches that you feel as if…"

"As if?"

"That it's really a dream," he said. He leaned closer and peered at something on the second-story porch. "Is that what I think it is?"

Camille laughed. "It wouldn't be the Winter Palace without your aunt Flora's beloved dog."

"She'll be delighted to know that Cornelius is immortalized in frosting," Maddox said. "It's perfect."

Camille's face tipped up to his, and the holiday window lights illuminated her eyes. She was also like a dream, something he knew he couldn't have but wanted so much. The look on her face shifted from playful to serious to something he could only describe as a question.

She reached up and placed a tiny, perfect kiss on his lips. "That was a thank-you for a nice evening."

He waited, lips parted, hoping she would do it again, but she turned her attention to the brightly lit window instead.

He reached for her hand and felt the warmth even through her gloves. He gave it a little squeeze. "Tonight was wonderful."

She nodded. "But I think it's time to turn out the lights and go home." She gave him one small smile and then took keys from her pocket and let herself into the candy store. A moment later, the lights in the display darkened, and he stood under the awning and felt the winter chill for the first time that evening.

CHAPTER FIFTEEN

CAMILLE STOOD IN the entrance of the horse barn while Cara finished brushing down a beautiful brown horse. All three of the Peterson daughters, and nearly everyone else on Christmas Island, knew how to ride a horse. Cars were the least popular form of transportation on the island. Instead, bikes, golf carts, sleds in the winter and horses year-round were preferred.

"It's already getting dark, and the old town hall is creepy at night," Cara said. "Maybe you could ask someone else to help you. How about Rebecca?"

"Rebecca's not from the island."

"That could be an advantage," Cara said.

"I see things as a historian, and you see things like a normal person," Camille told her sister Cara. "That's why I need your help."

Cara dropped her brush into a bucket and hung it on a peg. The horse barn housed a dozen horses, including two of Cara's that she earned free board for by doing chores and caring for the others. Camille had helped one summer when she was in high school, but the flies had driven her crazy. It was bad enough working taffy and fudge in the summer heat, but the candy shop had the great advantage of screens, whereas the horse barn left out the welcome mat for flies.

"You could ask Chloe? The two of you love the past, and I'm more of a present gal."

"I don't love the past in the same way Chloe does."

"Chloe saved every memento of her life in overflowing shoeboxes under her bed," Cara said, grinning and crossing her arms. "And you majored in history and then got entangled in the two-hundred-years-of-island-life project."

Camille had only one shoebox under her bed at her parents' house, and she'd forgotten to grab it when she moved to her downtown apartment. It had high school mementos in it, but she couldn't name most of the items in the box, no matter how important they had seemed at the time. Her graduation tassel was probably in there, and maybe a report card or an edition of the school newspaper. A memory of a pressed daisy came to mind. Maddox had given her that and she'd tucked it among some items. It might be in there, its petals turned to dust.

"Those are very different things," Camille said. "I'm interested in the past academically. Chloe is attached to the past in a sentimental way."

"Huge difference," Cara said. She ran a tap on the wall and filled a bucket, which she hauled over to a white horse with a black nose. She stroked the horse's nose affectionately. "That's what I love about horses. They live for the moment." The horse nudged Cara's pocket. "And for the sugar I swipe from the store," she added.

"Are you finished for the night?" Camille asked.

Cara blew her long bangs away from her face. "What the heck. I'm already dusty. How much dustier can I get pawing through old pictures in the town hall?"

"I knew you'd say yes. It's creepy in there at night, did you know that?"

Cara swatted Camille's arm and laughed as they both got in Cara's golf cart and drove downtown. The town hall building was on a street right behind the row of shops, hotels and restaurants. Tourists seldom noticed it, but it was the home of the police and fire departments with their limited fleet of vehicles in the garage behind the small white building. Most of the building served as a police station and meeting room, and a long, narrow room on the back held the town's history in crates and bins.

Camille let them in with the key that Shirley from the Chamber of Commerce had given her. Folding tables and chairs were the only furniture aside from the bookcases and shelves in the dark-paneled room.

"So, you're looking for stuff for next summer already?" Cara asked. "I thought you were planning to wait until winter, when things slow down?"

"If I have my way with my candy plans, things aren't going to slow down. And, besides, I'm really interested in this," Camille said.

"Where do you even start?" Cara asked.

"I'm thinking ahead to the bicentennial,

but tonight I'm looking for ideas for the May brothers. They've asked for my help with a little project."

"They?"

"Well, Maddox specifically, but it's a joint project."

Cara raised both eyebrows and leaned against a bookcase.

"They're building a passenger depot in Lakeside and want people to have something interesting to look at while they wait for the ferry," Camille explained. "Maddox asked me to put together a collection of photos he could have reproduced and framed."

Cara smiled but said nothing.

"What?" Camille asked. "It's a really nice idea."

"And very handy for him that he happens to know someone acquainted with… history."

"You're being ridiculous. Our past relationship has nothing to do with this. In fact, maybe I'll call him and ask him to join us so you can see he has a purely historical interest in this project."

Cara laughed. "That's a great idea. Then

I can leave and he can protect you from ghosts or spiders or whatever else you'll find in this dungeon."

Camille picked up her phone and texted Maddox to ask if he had time to meet her and Cara to give her a clearer sense of his plans. While she waited for a response, she scanned the labels on the front of a filing cabinet. The dates listed were decades old, and she pulled open a drawer to see what kinds of historical artifacts someone had saved from 1932 to 1945.

Her phone pinged, and Cara glanced up from her perusal of old ledgers that appeared to have come from a hotel or a bank. "Got company coming?"

Camille read the screen. "In half an hour. I better lay out a variety of pictures on these tables so I can see what he likes."

With Cara's help, Camille sorted through stacks of photographs. Someone had chosen to organize the shelves by theme instead of year. There was a nature theme, a boat theme, a winter theme and an island residents batch of photos.

"I like people pictures the most," Camille said. "I love seeing what they're wearing, what objects they're holding and what's in the background."

She chose a picture of three little girls on what was probably their first day of school. They stood in front of the current school building, but it looked different with its original wood siding and dirt walkway. The girls appeared to be sisters, each of them with a similar dress and their hair pulled up into a bow. One held a small chalkboard, one had a pencil and the smallest clutched a doll and looked as if she was going to cry.

Camille and Cara exchanged a smile. "That could've been us back in the day," Cara said. She dug through the pile and found pictures of downtown merchants and island visitors. "I wonder if there are some of our family?" she said. "That would actually be interesting."

Camille continued to lay out pictures, imagining a theme for the collections she would frame and hang in the passenger depot. Soon enough, she sensed someone standing in the door before Maddox spoke.

"I've never been in here," he said.

"Yes, you have. We came here on a

school field trip in third grade, because the social studies theme for that grade level was local history."

"Maybe I was absent that day," Maddox said.

Camille shook her head. "I remember walking with you from the school. I would have noticed if you weren't there."

They stared at each other a moment, and Camille wondered what Maddox had thought of her impulsive kiss several nights earlier under the candy shop's awning. She'd lain awake that night regretting it. Not only was it inviting trouble, but the kiss had awakened something very dangerous in her.

Feelings that weren't as dormant as she'd tried to believe. They were in grave danger of coming alive, and there was no way she was foolish enough to let that happen.

Cara cleared her throat. "I see you drove your truck," she said as she looked out the window.

"Are you thinking of stealing it?" Maddox asked with a smile.

"I'm thinking of asking you to give Camille a ride home so I can take the golf cart and escape this island graveyard."

"I don't need a ride," Camille said. "My apartment is two blocks away."

"But I will stay and make sure you don't stay up all night geeking out on history," Maddox said. "If you want me to."

"It won't take that long to show you what I'm considering for your displays, and you can let me know if I'm on the right track," Camille said.

"Thanks for getting started on this so soon, even though our new depot is just in the planning stages."

Camille gave a little shrug. "Just one island businessperson with big ideas trying to help out another one in the same boat."

"Looks like you two have this under control," Cara said. "Good night." She waved and left, closing the door behind her.

Camille saw the headlights of the golf cart sweep the side of the building and pierce through the dusty window, and then she was alone with Maddox.

"Why did you kiss me?" he asked.

Camille's heart thudded at his opening question. He could have asked about her day or spoken of the weather, but he went straight to the issue.

"To thank you for a nice evening," she said. She turned to the table of pictures and began organizing them by size, because her thoughts were too muddled to think about the content of the photographs.

"You're the one who paid for dinner," he said. He came over and laid a hand on top of one of her piles of pictures.

"Then I wanted to thank you for saving my father's life. He said he was nearly swept away and you pulled him back onto the boat." She glanced up, and his chin was too close. She could almost brush a kiss along the edge of his jaw without moving. His eyes were dark in the low light.

"You're welcome," he said. "I would have done that for anyone."

"Well, he's not just anyone to me."

"Me neither," Maddox said.

Camille stepped back and walked around the table so the wooden surface was between them. "I got an idea from the way these were organized. We could do groups of photographs in themes instead of a more traditional timeline. I think it will be more interesting to people."

"Whatever you think."

Surrounded by history, Camille was going to keep it where it belonged. In the past. No matter how…comfortable…she was becoming with Maddox again. Their personal history had not been all sunlit walks on school field trips.

"I think one grouping on island nature and natural landmarks would be good, but people really want to see something they can identify with, like people having fun frolicking in the water or riding bicycles down Holly Street. Your history idea is good, but often people want something more." She held up black-and-white pictures of people wearing clothing from early in the previous century. Their bicycles were old-fashioned, as was their clothing, but their faces and smiles could have belonged in the current year. People weren't so different, even if their circumstances were.

"I love this one," she said. She held out a picture for him. It was a child standing in front of the Island Candy and Fudge shop. The child was crying and pointing to the store. "Do you think she has a toothache or she's crying because her mother won't buy her candy?"

"The latter, I hope. It makes a better story. It's funny how much that place hasn't changed. I would recognize it even if it weren't for the sign."

Camille sighed. "That's the idea. It's a very traditional business, or at least it was until I came along with my refrigerated truck and distribution center in Lakeside."

Maddox handed back the picture of the crying child. "But you kept the history even if you added a bunch of…future."

"And I'm planning to add a lot more," Camille said. It was a good opportunity to reinforce the fact that she had plenty of future plans, just in case he might be thinking that she could be sucked back into the past. She had been holding her breath as she waited to see how the Halloween and Christmas orders would go, but it was becoming more clear every day that she had a winner in her online marketing and branching-out plans. "I'm not crazy about that delivery truck, and if I convert my warehouse in Lakeside to a production facility, I won't need the truck anymore. I can manufacture and ship from Lakeside and the candy won't have to get on the ferry at all."

"How will you manage all that from here?"

She shrugged and straightened a stack of pictures. "I may have to be there a lot."

Maddox's expression sobered. "That's disappointing."

"You'll hardly miss the money my tickets are bringing in. Your business will double without my truck taking up space on your ferry."

"I mean it's disappointing that you might be spending so much time in Lakeside. I thought you came back because you wanted to be on Christmas Island."

"I came back to grow my family's business," she said.

Maddox swallowed and searched her face for a moment, but he didn't say anything. She wondered if a part of him thought she'd come back for him. Did he imagine she would throw away a business opportunity because of a sentimental attachment to the island or the past? She'd left once and stayed away for seven years.

One kiss—no matter how much she might have enjoyed it—was not going to change her future trajectory. She was done answering to anyone. That was the reason she'd come back when she did. It was Camille's turn to shine without sharing the spotlight with Chloe. She owed herself the opportunity to prove she wasn't anyone's second choice—especially the man standing in front of her.

"I want you to do whatever you want," Maddox said.

Camille wasn't sure if he was talking about her declaration regarding her candy business or the plans for a history display in his passenger depot.

Maddox walked over to a shelf where a model ship gathered dust among other items. "Do you think there are any pictures of ferry boats from a long time ago? I'd like to see those. The ferry we're running right now has been in use since I was Ethan's age. I remember Mom taking me and Griffin down to the dock to watch Dad bring the ferry across for the first time."

"That must have made quite an impression," Camille said. She remembered similar milestones in her family's candy business. A kitchen remodel, a new front counter that ran perpendicular to the old one and opened up the space more. She could still remember the store exactly how it was when she was in kindergarten, and she remembered the winter they remodeled right after they took down the Christmas decorations.

"It did," Maddox said. "And I would never have believed then that Griffin and I would be running it together now."

"Didn't you always think you would take over the family business? I thought I remembered you talking about it."

Maddox ran a finger along the bow of the model ship. "I always thought of it as a someday thing. When I was old like my parents. I didn't think it would be basically the only thing I would ever do."

Camille felt her heart sink. His tone implied that he was disappointed with the way his life had turned out. Since high school, she'd focused on her own anger and hurt at his betrayal, but did he feel as if he'd betrayed himself?

"But you lived in Lakeside for a while, didn't you?" She didn't want to hear the details of his marriage and had carefully avoided thinking about how he'd spent his days in the years after she left the island.

"I technically lived there, but I worked on the ferry and went back and forth. I tried to make it work, but it was clear that my efforts weren't enough for the family business or my marriage."

"I'm sorry," Camille said, her heart aching unexpectedly for him.

He shook his head. "Don't be. My marriage was doomed from the start because I—"

Camille held her breath, wanting but dreading to hear his next words.

"I was in love with someone else."

He looked up and met her eyes, and his were so full of pain that she wanted to go to him and comfort him, but she couldn't. She'd worked too hard to get past the place where their past relationship had the power to hurt her ever again, and she couldn't risk a word, a touch, a kiss.

Maddox shook his head, his jaw tight, and he walked out the door, leaving her with boxes and files full of hundreds of stories that might never get told.

CHAPTER SIXTEEN

MADDOX USUALLY LOVED the early-morning ferry runs, but he was happy to hand over the Saturday morning trip to his brother. The second weekend of December was full-on chaos on Christmas Island. Every mainlander within a one-hundred-mile radius came to the island for the annual Christmas festival. It was the last retail blast for island merchants and an opportunity to host tourists before the weather worsened as winter chill gripped northern Michigan.

"Lucky today," he told Griffin. "For December, this is practically a beach day."

"If you wear your long underwear to the beach," Griffin said. He pulled his dark knitted cap low over his head.

"You look like a longshoreman, and you didn't even shave this morning. You'll scare the holiday revelers."

"Not if I stay in the nice warm pilothouse," Griffin said. "As soon as I unload the passengers, I'll meet you at the hotel. Rebecca's already there helping Hadley with the Christmas tree out front, so you may get lucky and not have much to do."

Maddox laughed. "There's always plenty to do at the last minute. Safe passage," he said and slapped his brother on the back. Maddox walked down Holly Street, noting the fresh evergreen trees lining the sides of the streets. The trees had their roots balled and would be replanted on the island, but first they'd welcome tourists for the Christmas festival.

"Ours is the best one already," Maddox said as he approached the Island Hotel, where his son was attempting to thread popcorn onto a string.

"It's for the birds," Ethan said, holding up the string.

"Let's hope they are polite and don't eat it until after the tourists have all gone home."

Next door, the bar was decorating its tree with bar napkins folded into birds of paradise and some bottle caps on strings catching the breeze.

"We should roll the baby grand out here so you could play for tourists," he told Rebecca as he helped her with an ornament near the top of the tree.

She shook her head. "The piano wouldn't like the change in temperature. I wouldn't want people to think I played off-key."

"I sing off-key," Maddox said, "but it's the intent that counts."

"What do you sing?"

Maddox turned at the sound of Camille's voice. It had only been a few days since he'd admitted to her that his marriage was a mistake. They hadn't seen each other since, and Maddox had felt his heart sink every time he replayed his words. He shouldn't have said them, shouldn't have picked at the scar.

"Whatever the occasion demands," he said. "Usually sea shanties because of my line of work."

Ethan giggled. "Dad sings silly songs while I'm in the bathtub and when he cooks stuff in the kitchen."

Maddox put his fingers over his son's

lips. "Don't give away all the family se-crets."

"I don't think I've ever heard you sing," Camille said. "Funny how you can spend so much time with someone and yet…"

Maddox smelled evergreen and heard laughter and even sleigh bells all around him, but all he could think about was Ca-mille. Her words were so raw and personal. Did she care that she'd never heard him sing, or was there something more to her statement?

Rebecca cleared her throat. "Ethan, do you know 'Jingle Bells'? We could go in-side and practice with the piano and then come back out and sing for the tourists."

"Okay," Ethan agreed.

Rebecca held out her hand, and they went inside.

"Would you like to hear a sea shanty?" Maddox asked when he was alone with Ca-mille. He didn't know what to say.

Camille smiled. "I should make you prove you weren't bluffing about that, but you should save your voice for the tour-ists. Rebecca is a good singer as well as an excellent piano player, so I wouldn't be surprised if she roped you into some caroling as the first wave of tourists rolls off the ferry."

"Same every year. Did you miss the utter insanity of the festival when you were away?" he asked.

"Only a little." Camille squared her shoulders, and her expression became all business instead of the soft, sentimental look of a moment earlier. "I came over to ask if you can run a ferry for me on Monday morning for my last Christmas shipment. I would pay fuel costs, of course. Or should I try to squeeze my truck on with the returning tourists on Sunday night?"

She'd only crossed the street and walked a block to ask about the ferry schedule. Not to see him. He should take a lesson from her ability to be matter-of-fact and unmoved by him. Except for that hug on the ferry dock. And the kiss a few nights after that. Was she really as divorced from the past as she claimed to be?

"The forecast is fine," he said. "And we were planning a package and parcel run on Monday so the Christmas deliveries don't bog down the mail plane too much. I think you can count on it, but I'll let you know tomorrow afternoon if you need to be on the boat."

"Thanks. I'm only making a few hundred pounds more fudge this weekend, and it's going to be my last stand before Christmas."

"What about your online shoppers?"

"I was very clear that the last guaranteed ship date before Christmas would be Monday. If people miss their opportunity, they miss out, plain and simple."

Maddox knew exactly what it felt like to destroy an opportunity. Had Camille also learned this the hard way? What did he really know about her life during the seven years she'd been gone? Had she dated, fallen in love? Was he the only man to have broken her heart…and had she broken some hearts, too?

Maybe they really were strangers who happened to share something that was clearly in the past. What about their futures, though? Christmas Island was small, and it seemed even smaller during the winter.

"What about after Christmas?" he asked. "Will you slow down?"

"My online sales won't, but if I remember correctly, the entire island slows to a dead stop after Christmas."

"I can't wait," Maddox said. He looked forward to working on his ferry expansion during the day and spending quiet evenings playing games or watching television with Ethan. Ice would eventually insulate the island from the outside world, and it would be a kind of peace you couldn't get anywhere else. He'd tried. Had she also found that there was no replacement for the solitude and community of the islanders brave enough to weather the winter season?

"I have to get back to my tree," Camille said. "We only have an hour until the ferry arrives, and people will expect a Christmas wonderland."

Maddox looked up at the white lights crossing the street, the wreaths on every lamppost, the window decorations and the dozens of live evergreens lining Holly Street. "That's exactly what they'll find," he said. "Pure magic."

Movement in front of the Island Candy and Fudge shop caught his eye. "Looks like reinforcements have arrived," he said, nodding in that direction.

Camille spun around. "Oh, no. Chloe." Her words sounded exasperated and frustrated.

"Is there a problem with Chloe decorating the tree? I imagine she's done it for the last seven years."

"Which is exactly why I get to do it this year. Chloe is leaving. The future of the shop is in my hands, not hers."

Maddox was surprised and a little shocked by the vehemence of Camille's words. Camille took a step off the curb and started forward, but Maddox shot out a hand and touched her sleeve.

"Wait."

Camille turned, arms crossed. "I have to get down there before it ends up covered in pink bows."

"Is it really about the pink bows and the tree?"

"Of course it is."

Maddox tilted his head. "It's been a while, but you used to confide in me when something was bothering you."

Camille's cheeks flushed hot pink. "You're

right. I told you everything. I gave you everything. And you threw it away." She spun and took long strides down the street.

A sleigh pulled by a single white horse passed by, and Santa waved at all the islanders out decorating their storefronts and business.

"I'm sorry," Maddox yelled as he hurried to catch up with her. "All right? I'm sorry. I'm sorry a million times over."

Camille put up a hand and kept walking.

"You know what, Camille? For someone who claims she's not all bogged down in the past, you sure have a hard time letting go of it."

Christmas music began playing over a loudspeaker, but not before Camille and probably a dozen other people had heard him.

She turned around slowly, and Maddox felt the kind of fear usually reserved for massive waves rolling over the front of his boat and threatening to send him to a watery grave.

"How. Dare. You," she enunciated, snapping off each word. "How dare you lecture me on what is worth holding on to and what isn't? You," she said, jabbing her finger at him, "you are the one who destroyed everything we had. You drove me away. It took me seven long years to think I could stand the sight of you again."

"Did I really drive you away? What if you had stayed and fought for what we had? You dropped me over a single kiss and got out of here like you couldn't leave fast enough."

"Are you kidding? You wanted me to stay and humiliate myself while you married your weekend fling?"

Maddox started to say something, but then he remembered his son and checked to see that he was still inside. Ethan didn't need to overhear this.

Mercifully, Ethan was nowhere to be found. Rebecca was probably playing every fun Christmas song in her big book, and Ethan was almost certainly singing along in his sweet little voice. Maddox began walking back toward his hotel, his son, his future.

"Are you just going to walk away?" Camille called after him.

He paused and turned. "I can't change

the past. My son's in there, and he's my future." He turned his back on Camille and took the steps into his hotel two at a time.

"Do I EVEN want to know what just happened?" Cara asked.

"I'll tell you what just happened," Camille said, her breath heaving. Despite the brisk winter day, her face was hot as July. She couldn't believe the things he'd had the nerve to say to her, and she was amazed at herself for firing back. "I told him off and ended it with him."

Cara bit her lower lip and tilted her head. The string of white lights in her hands drooped.

"You know what I mean," Camille huffed.

"You ended it with Maddox seven years ago."

"I left seven years ago." Maddox had the audacity to claim that she was the one who had slammed the door on their relationship by leaving, and that she should have stayed and fought. It was beyond outrageous.

"Because…you ended it," Cara said. "That's how that works, right?"

"I left because I wanted to leave." She'd

been planning all along to leave the island at the end of the summer and go to college. She'd imagined a tearful farewell to Maddox and her family at the ferry dock and then the happy reunion scenes when she returned at holidays and for the summer. But she had hardly returned in all those years. And there had been no tearful scenes.

Cara nodded slowly. "Maybe you should take a moment and regroup. Go in the back of the store where no one can see you and eat chocolate icing with a spoon. Chloe and I have the tree and storefront under control."

"Of course you do. Perfect Chloe will make the perfect tree. Better than I would have, I'm sure."

Cara reached down, scooped up handfuls of snow and shaped a snowball. She handed the snowball to Camille. "Throw it. As hard as you can. Throw it at the sky, a person, the front of a building, I don't care. And I'm going to keep handing you snowballs and you're going to keep throwing them until you've pulled yourself together."

Camille stared at the snowball. She turned around and glared at the Holiday

Hotel, which was across the street and down a block. Out of her range. But she could still try. She wound up and threw the snowball as hard as she could, just as the sleigh with Santa made another pass through downtown. Her snowball hit Santa squarely in the back of his red suit, and he lost his balance and almost fell off the sleigh.

Camille put her hands over her face, her wet gloves cooling her cheeks. "Oh, my goodness."

"I hope you feel better," Cara said. "You were being a petulant child anyway, so pelting Santa with a snowball probably isn't going to get you much farther down the naughty list."

"I wasn't being a child."

Cara shaped another snowball and handed it to her. "You were. Chloe was daughter number one forever. Big deal. She's out. You're the candy queen now. And the only person doubting that is you."

Camille's mouth dropped open. "What?" Her younger sister had always been the mild-mannered member of the family, never joining in a family argument, never taking sides.

Cara continued shaping snowballs and handing them over until Camille's hands were full of wintry weapons. She jammed one last snowball into Camille's hands.

"You heard me," Cara said. "No one thinks you can't pull this off, unless you do. Which makes you the only no vote. So get over yourself."

Camille threw a snowball at her younger sister and tagged her in the back as she bent down to make a fresh snowball. The snow went down the back of Cara's neck, and she stood up and tried to shake it off.

"Feel better?" Cara asked.

"Getting there."

"Good," Cara said. She pelted Camille with a snowball.

"I thought I was supposed to be throwing those."

"You are," Cara said, hitting her with another throw.

A snowball hit Camille from the side, and she turned to see Rebecca and Ethan laughing while Ethan packed another snowball.

"My best friend, too?"

Rebecca shrugged. "It looked like you were having fun."

Camille threw a snowball at Rebecca while being simultaneously hit with two others. The island residents who were supposed to be putting the final touches on their Christmas trees and storefronts poured into the street and joined in the battle. Camille shaped and threw snowballs as fast as she could, taking fire from all sides and returning it. She didn't know when Maddox had joined the fight, but she noticed him when she saw a snowball hurtling toward her face until it was swiped away by a black glove at the very last minute.

"Face shots are illegal," he said. "Too personal."

Camille lowered her throwing arm. "Thank you."

He spread his arms in a gesture of surrender. "Do you want to take a shot at me? I'm open."

Camille considered it. Two minutes earlier, she would have fired with all her might, but the cathartic snowball fight was working its magic, and she could admit Maddox was just a little bit correct about letting go of the past. She smiled. "No, thanks."

A snowball caught Maddox in the back of the head, and he swayed toward her. "It's getting brutal out here."

"I'm afraid I may have started it when I winged Santa."

"You're getting coal in your stocking."

She giggled. "It was almost worth it."

Maddox laughed, and they stood smiling at each other while snowballs filled the air around them. Maybe, Camille thought, just maybe they could be friends again.

"They're here," someone yelled. "The ferry!"

The snowballs stopped flying, and the crowd scattered. In just minutes, hundreds of people, the full capacity of the ferry, would stroll down Holly Street in pursuit of the magic of the holiday. Camille turned toward her candy store just in time to watch Chloe tie a bright pink ribbon to the top of the evergreen out front.

Camille sighed. Next year she would take control of the decorations.

CHAPTER SEVENTEEN

LATE ON SUNDAY, as darkness covered Christmas Island and the downtown lights created an oasis of holiday warmth, the business owners breathed a collective happy sigh as the weekend shoppers and revelers made their way to the last ferry. Camille took off her apron and looped it over a peg behind the sales register at the Island Candy and Fudge shop.

"One of us should go drag Chloe back for the sing-along," Cara said. "She walked with Dan to the dock to wave goodbye for the week, and she's probably going to be all watery."

"The caroling will cheer her up," Camille said.

"Only if she goes and one of us helps buffer some of the…emotion," Cara said. "I can't wait until her wedding is over and we can all get off the roller coaster."

AMIE DENMAN 273

"The roller coaster's not so bad as long as we're on the sides watching it."

Cara flashed a sarcastic smile. "You don't live at home. You retreat to your apartment that is so not pink and pretty and doesn't have a single scrap of lace or a tearstain anywhere."

"I know." Camille grinned. "I'm the lucky one."

"Can I come live with you?"

"Only one bedroom," Camille said. "But you can hide out on my couch anytime, and I'll be nice and go down to the dock to retrieve Chloe and bring her back for the singing."

Camille put on her red wool coat and trooped down the street. The shops were still lit, decorations aglow, and music came from all around her. She could see the ferry at the end of the street with its boarding lights illuminating the deck. There had to be three hundred people making the return to the mainland.

The ferry's departure horn sounded, clashing with the pretty Christmas music on the street behind her. As she approached, she saw only a few people standing onshore. One of them was Chloe, who was waving to the departing ferry. Camille strained her eyes and saw Dan standing at the railing, waving back. She sighed and felt a rush of sympathy for the two lovers being separated, even for just a week and even though soon they'd be married and living together. No wonder Chloe felt weepy and a bit torn apart lately.

In addition to a few other people waving from shore, Maddox was watching the ferry depart. He secured a line at the edge of the dock and then turned and saw Camille approaching.

"We survived another Christmas festival weekend," he said, smiling when he saw her. All the islanders felt the same way about the wildly busy second weekend in December. The business and spirit were fantastic, but it was a two-day marathon, not to mention the work preparing for it. Skipper padded up, sniffed Camille's glove and then sat next to his owner.

"We did," Camille agreed as she found a piece of broken cookie in her pocket for the golden. "I came to collect my sister and make sure she goes to the sing-along, just in case she needs cheering up."

"I did notice some tears as Dan got on the ferry."

Camille nodded. "I'm sure. But cookies and hot chocolate will help. You're coming, right?"

"I'm waiting here for Griffin to get back. I'll help him dock and secure everything for the night, and then we'll come down to the park and join in the singing. We've given everyone else the night off."

"Where's Ethan?" Camille asked.

"Rebecca is taking him. She's great with him and, honestly, has been a lifesaver for me a few times."

"There's a reason she's my best friend."

"She said you'd told her all about the island sing-along, and she's looking forward to it."

"It's one of the things I've missed most. Although I'll admit that list is pretty long."

Maddox met her eyes, and they didn't say anything for a moment. The ferry's lights were growing dimmer, and Camille saw her sister drop her arm and dig through her pockets for a tissue.

"I have to get back to the store and help my parents clean and lock up, and then I'll bring some treats to the park. If anything's left in the display cases. That was a really fun crowd this weekend."

"We ran three round trips each day, each of them almost at capacity, which is five hundred passengers," Maddox said. "That's a lot of people, but I'm still running the morning ferry if you have any fudge and candy left to ship tomorrow."

"Plenty. I made and boxed the orders ahead of time. I'll be the first one on the ferry."

Camille held out an arm for Chloe as she approached, and she shoulder-hugged her sister. "Dan was brave about the ferry," Camille said. "I know he hates water, but that means he must really love you, right?"

Chloe nodded, and Camille smiled a goodbye to Maddox and turned to walk her sister back to the candy store. Chloe's slight limp, a leftover from a childhood broken leg, was more noticeable than usual, something that only happened when she was distracted. "Doing okay?" Camille asked. She was used to Chloe sharing her thoughts and feelings freely, so the silence was concerning. Was she just tired after the long weekend?

As soon as they finished their short, silent walk and entered the brightly lit candy store, Chloe grabbed a broom and began sweeping, head down, focused on her work. Camille went to the computer to run sales reports while keeping a curious watch on her older sister.

"Is something wrong with your sister?" her dad whispered.

"I noticed she's pretty quiet," Camille said.

"She's sweeping the floor. I've never seen her do that," he said.

Camille and her dad exchanged a raised-eyebrow look.

"She'll feel better after the sing-along. If I remember right, it's the best night of the year," Camille said. "And we have a lot to celebrate, if my first glance at these sales figures is right. It looks like our highest sales day outside of the summer season."

"Good weather for people to cross the lake," her dad said. "And you've really been getting our name out there." He smiled at her. "I'm sure at least a thousand of the weekend visitors came just for our candy shop."

Camille laughed. "That's a nice idea, but I think they came because it's Christmas Island and this festival is legendary."

She'd also asked the May brothers to hand out a coupon with each ferry ticket they sold. The drawer by the register was jammed full of the pink coupons for 15 percent discounts on candy. She had asked both Griffin and Maddox for permission, and Camille knew it was also to her benefit that her best friend was now the business manager for the ferry line. It was one more way her path was going to cross with Maddox's, and she didn't want to read too much into that. That was life on the island. Restaurant owners partnered with hotels; shop owners partnered with each other. They all knew each other's names and what was new in their business and personal lives.

Thirty minutes later, Camille's family met in the downtown park. In the summer, green lawn swept down to the lake, where a community harbor held hundreds of sailboats and powerboats. This evening, snow crunched underfoot and white lights stretched overhead. Red lights encircled the park's trees, and laughter and the smell of hot chocolate filled the air.

"Jordan and I got roped into leading the singing," Violet said as she came up and put an arm around Camille.

Camille smiled at her friend. "You two harmonize well together, and I hope the rest of us don't ruin the music."

"Just sing loud. And I'm keeping it to ten songs only so we can eat cookies and then go home and collapse."

"Busy weekend in the boutique?"

"The busiest since summer. Good, though. I had some awesome holiday dresses that I was glad to see find a home," Violet said. She turned and smiled. "Who's your handsome date, Rebecca?"

Rebecca held Ethan's hand as she came up to them. "I found this sailor down by the docks and thought he could use some holiday cheer."

Ethan giggled, and the hot chocolate in his cup sloshed over the side. "Can we do 'Jingle Bells'?"

"Of course," Violet said.

Violet went up onto the bandstand with Jordan, and she held up a hand to get the crowd's attention. As Camille looked around, she saw nearly a hundred locals, all of whom she knew. Some of them had moved to the island during the seven years she'd been gone, but she'd gotten to know them since returning the island in June. She could hardly believe she'd been back six whole months. The time had flown. Before she knew it, she'd be her parents' age, still living in her downtown apartment, where she'd hardly unpacked.

"We're starting with 'Jingle Bells' as a special request," Jordan called. He and Violet hummed a key and began singing cheerfully. As Camille watched them, she wondered how they could possibly not see that their harmony extended beyond music. Would their friendship someday blossom into love…and then sink or swim? Camille wasn't sure, but she and Maddox were, at least, afloat again.

Violet and Jordan led the group through "Jolly Old Saint Nicholas," and Camille saw Griffin and Maddox joining the circle as the song ended. Maddox smiled at

Rebecca and claimed his son's hand. Camille felt as though the circle of islanders was complete now, and her eyes got a little watery as they sang "White Christmas" together. Although the song was sentimental and serious, Camille laughed when Skipper joined in and howled through part of a verse. Maddox put a hand on Skipper's snout, but Camille had a better idea. She took the rest of the broken cookie from her pocket and offered it to the dog, who preferred the treat to singing.

People around them chuckled at the sight, but Camille glanced over at her family and noticed that her sister Chloe was not laughing. She was crying. Not sentimental tears brought on by the sweet holiday song, but sad crying. Bordering on sobbing.

Camille felt someone nudge her, and a second later she felt warm breath on her cheek and ear. "Is your sister okay?" Maddox asked.

"I don't know," Camille said, turning her head a fraction. Her cheek brushed his, and Camille felt a rush of emotion. *It's just the holiday and the singing*, she thought.

"Is there anything I can do?" he asked.

Camille pulled back just enough to look into his eyes, which were sweet and sincere. Everyone around them was singing "I'll Be Home for Christmas," but all Camille wanted to do was freeze the moment when she and Maddox were close enough to touch and she smelled lake water and damp wool, the fragrances that always clung to him during the winter. He hadn't taken time to shave during the busy weekend, and the stubble on his chin tickled her cheek and reminded her how ruggedly handsome he was now instead of the boyishly handsome he'd been years ago.

How much had she changed? What did he think of her now versus then?

She wanted to ask, but she couldn't. She shook her head. "Thanks, but I better find out what's wrong with Chloe. Maybe it's nothing."

"It doesn't look like nothing," Maddox said.

Camille swallowed and ducked behind her parents so she could take Chloe's arm and lead her away from the group without everyone noticing.

"What's the matter?" she said quietly as

the group continued singing. They moved behind an evergreen covered in twinkling red lights.

"I'm calling off my wedding," Chloe choked out. She swiped at her tears with the back of her mittened hand. "I can't get married and leave."

"Yes, you can," Camille said. "You love Dan. Your wedding is in three weeks."

Chloe shook her head. "No. I was perfectly happy before I met him. I love my life here. I don't want to change everything."

Camille pulled her sister into a hug and let her cry all over her wool coat while she listened to her fellow islanders sing "Silent Night." She took a deep breath and released it very slowly to keep herself from crying, too. What should she say to her sister? Get married even if you don't want to? Call off your wedding to a perfectly wonderful guy just because you have cold feet? The exhaustion from a busy weekend and the emotion of the season was getting to them. That was all.

Even though she wore her heavy winter boots, Camille's feet were freezing, but it was the literal kind, not like Chloe's. If her sister didn't get married and leave, would she expect to have everything stay status quo? Camille knew there was no going back and recapturing things that were in the past, which was one of the very good reasons she was keeping her head clear about her friend Maddox. There was no way to jump back seven and a half years, even if she wanted to.

"Have you told Dan you're having second thoughts?" Camille asked.

She felt her sister shake her head.

That, at least, was a relief. There was no harm done. Yet. And if Chloe stayed, would she want to keep running the candy business? Where would that leave Camille? She berated herself for thinking selfish thoughts as she held her sister and let her cry on her shoulder. The last strains of "Silent Night" ended, and Camille knew everyone would move toward the coffee and cookie station set up on a picnic table. If would be only minutes before they were missed and their mother or Cara came looking.

"What's going on?" Camille's mother

asked as she came around the evergreen and almost bumped into them. "What's the matter?"

"Cold feet," Camille said.

Melinda kissed the back of Chloe's head. "Let's go home where it's warm and we can talk about this."

Camille had planned to retreat to her nearby apartment and take a long hot shower after the busy weekend, but she couldn't abandon her sister when she was having an emotional crisis. It was part of being a family, and she vividly remembered how her family had taken her side without asking any questions that long-ago summer when her own heart was breaking.

MADDOX KEPT ONE eye on his son and the other on Camille and Chloe. He felt sorry for Camille, trying to juggle her family issues while also working so hard on her business goals. She'd always been an overachiever, working hard in her classes, at the store, driving herself. He'd been the opposite as a teenager, letting life come to him. If he could advise his own son which route to take, he'd probably tell him to find a happy medium. Life had come to Maddox, but he should have worked harder to be ready for it and deserve it.

As the music ended, he saw Chloe walk away with her parents and Cara trailing behind. Camille stayed for a moment to go to the dessert table and collect the trays and containers she'd brought filled with cookies and holiday treats. Maddox took Ethan's hand and walked over to the table that was absolutely loaded with temptation.

"Only two things," he told his son. "I know you've had sugary treats all weekend, and you have to go to sleep tonight, because you have school tomorrow."

Camille smiled at Ethan. "That's good advice. And if you only get two things, I'm going to suggest this." She pointed at a huge gingerbread cookie colorfully decorated and embellished with tiny bits of candy. "And this." She held up a red-, green- and white-striped candy cane. "We pulled the sugar and made it ourselves at the shop. It's the best candy cane you'll ever have."

"Wow," Ethan said, his eyes huge as he looked at the giant candy cane.

"I'd eat the cookie and have hot chocolate tonight, and then I think you should save the candy cane for a treat after school tomorrow."

"You do?"

She nodded. "I'm an expert on candy, remember?"

"Okay."

Ethan took the gingerbread cookie, sat on a nearby bench and began eating. A moment later, a girl his age joined him on the bench, also with a cookie in her hand.

"Is everything okay with your family?" Maddox asked.

Camille sighed and walked off to the side with him where they weren't likely to be overheard. "Chloe is having a moment. She says she's calling off her wedding."

"Did something…bad happen?"

What if Dan had been unkind to her or, worse, cheated on her? Chloe deserved better than that. Every woman did. Talking about a terrible breakup was dangerous territory for the friendship they seemed to be rekindling. He hoped that, somehow, by bringing their own breakup into the light earlier in the day, it might have somehow put it to rest.

"Nothing happened," Camille said. "That I know of. I think the holiday festivities have gotten to her and she has cold feet. We all know this is the best place in the world at Christmastime."

"All the time," Maddox said.

"But especially Christmas, with all the emotions. Chloe loves everything just as it is and is afraid to change, even for true love, I guess."

"Change is scary," Maddox said. "Even good change."

"I'm not so sure about that. I'm making huge changes in our candy business, and you don't see me crying behind Christmas trees."

"That's not the same," Maddox said. "And you can't tell me there aren't times when you're scared to death you're making the wrong move."

Camille shoved her hands in her pockets and looked away from him, her jaw set.

"Maybe it's just me, then. I get night sweats just thinking about how we're going to run two ferries next year on top of the hotel and whatever other expansion plans I agree to."

Camille's shoulders lowered just a little. He was happy to admit his own fears and failures, but he'd learned that lesson the hard way. It wasn't fair to assume Camille had the same fears and worries. She had experience running a big candy business in Chicago.

Rebecca came over. "Sorry to interrupt, but I'm worried about your sister. I saw her crying."

"Cold feet over her wedding," Camille said.

"You're kidding. You always told me those stories about how she played bride with lace curtains, tablecloths, even bedsheets. She's been looking forward to her wedding day all her life."

Camille smiled. "I think the reality of leaving the island and everyone she knows is setting in."

Rebecca nodded. "That's really hard."

Camille reached out and squeezed her friend's arm. "I should go and do my part to help her through this."

"Are you going to persuade her to get married?"

Maddox watched Camille's face where he could see in the lines of her mouth that she was really conflicted about her answer.

"No one should get married unless they are absolutely sure it's the best thing for both of them."

It would be unfair to read too much into her statement. He knew from hard experience that people get married for all kinds of reasons and results varied.

"But what are we going to do with her if she stays?" Camille said with a half smile.

"I see what you mean," Rebecca said quietly.

"She can help you build the candy empire," Maddox said. He thought this was the right answer until he saw Camille's smile fade fast.

"Ships don't need two captains," she said.

"Sure they do. It can—"

"I have to go," she said.

Camille turned and walked away, leaving Maddox and Rebecca watching her.

"Did I say the wrong thing somehow?" he asked. "You know Camille as well as anybody, and I think I screwed that up even though I was trying to help."

Rebecca sighed. "You're not wrong about the two captains thing, but think about Camille's position. She finally came home to lead the family business because her perfect older sister was leaving. The timing was no accident. If Chloe doesn't leave, Camille is back to being number two." Rebecca held up two fingers to emphasize her words.

"But her family has to see how hard she's working and how much candy she's selling."

"It doesn't matter what they think. It matters what she thinks. It's not fun coming in second place."

Maddox rolled his shoulders. "I'm the second child in my family, and Griffin and I don't have any issues sharing the business."

Rebecca cocked her head. "Was it always that way?"

Maddox felt his heart sink, and he shook his head slowly. "No," he admitted. "For a long time, Griffin was the good son, and I was the one who screwed up his life and then had to fight to put it back together."

"And you did," Rebecca said. "You two are an amazing partnership."

"So, Chloe and Camille could do the same thing."

Rebecca smiled. "Every family is different. That's something I learned from living with so many different families as a foster kid. You have to figure out where you belong in the mix, and if you don't like your place, you have to figure out how to change it. Camille's working on it, probably harder than she needs to, but she has to figure that out for herself."

Something nagged at Maddox as he gathered up Ethan and took him home. Rebecca had said so many things that gave him food for thought, but one in particular hit him like a brick. *It's not fun coming in second place.* He'd put Camille in second place once, and he wished he could go back and change it.

CHAPTER EIGHTEEN

MADDOX WATCHED ETHAN enter the island school building with a mixture of relief and sadness. Caring for a six-year-old was exhausting. Just that morning, Ethan had tossed his sneaker for the dog to catch and then cried when his shoe came back wet with chew marks. Aside from snow boots and slippers, Maddox realized, his son only had a pair of shiny black dress shoes in addition to the sneakers he wore to school. And the dress shoes were too small.

Being a single parent was full of mornings like that, but it was also full of indescribable joy and sweetness, like the hug his son gave him before he got out of the pickup and the way Ethan turned around and waved one more time before he went through the school door. Those were the things that tugged at Maddox's heart as he realized the boy was getting older every day, and those hugs and waves would slow down and eventually disappear.

He drove to the ferry dock and began his morning precheck on the mechanical and safety aspects of the vessel. Whether they were at full capacity with hundreds of people on board or just himself and Skipper, the boat didn't leave the dock without every assurance it would return. His dog followed him through his rounds, and they emerged from the engine house in time to see Camille's giant truck pulling onto the dock. Her blond hair shone through the windshield, and Maddox smiled. He didn't know anyone with her persistence. He just wished she would be interested in renewing their relationship with the same persistence she did everything else. But...what would he do if she wanted that? Was it wise to risk a relationship now when he had so many other changes in his life? Would it be best for his son?

He waved her onto the boat and pointed to the place he wanted her to park for balance. There were six other passengers with ferry tickets, all of them overnight guests at his and Griffin's hotel. They'd chosen to stay another night when they heard there would be a special ferry. When Rebecca heard about it, she suggested they make a practice of offering a Monday morning ferry after the Christmas festival as a way to encourage more business.

"You control the ferry, which gives you a lot of power. You should use it wisely," she'd said.

Maddox hadn't thought much about the influence he and Griffin could exert. They'd always considered their ferry to be a service to the island, but Rebecca was right. Although there were so many things he couldn't control, Maddox was glad this was one he could.

"Thanks again," Camille said as she turned off the truck and slid out of the driver's seat. Her bag got caught on her coat's zipper and followed her out of the truck, spilling its contents on the ferry floor.

Maddox knelt and helped her scoop up her phone, some papers, a bottle of water and an insulated lunch box. The sight of the lunch box jogged a memory, and he stood up quickly. The feeling he'd forgotten something had been nagging him since he got to the dock. "Oh, rats," he said.

"What?" Camille asked as she zipped the bag and shoved it onto the truck's seat.

"Ethan's lunch. I have the sinking feeling he left his lunch box in the truck when I dropped him off at school."

"Oh," Camille said. "Will he have to eat school lunch in the cafeteria?"

Maddox shook his head. "He doesn't like that. He says he likes what I make for him."

"He has high standards," Camille said.

Maddox smiled. "I make the same thing every day, so I don't really think so, but he's already having a tough day. The dog tried to eat his shoe."

Camille followed him as he walked the short distance to his truck and saw the evidence on the floor. Ethan's blue lunch box with a cartoon character on it was on the floor of the truck.

Camille put a hand on his arm. "It'll be okay," she said.

Maddox looked at his watch. It would take him ten minutes to drive to the island school to drop off the lunch. The ferry would hardly be late, and Camille would tell the other passengers to wait. But he couldn't leave the ferry running and the dock unattended.

"Give me your keys," Camille said.

"To the boat?"

She laughed. "To your truck. If you promise not to leave without me, I'll take Ethan's lunch to the school."

"Really?"

"Of course."

Maddox reached into his coat pocket for the truck keys. "Thank you. You're a lifesaver."

"I'm hardly saving a life. I'm dropping off the gourmet lunch you labored over."

"It's a peanut butter and honey sandwich, an apple, pretzels and half of the candy cane you gave him last night."

Camille smiled. "Excellent. I'd happily eat that if someone loved me enough to make it for me every day."

Maddox felt his breath catch at the way she put that. He'd make her a lunch every day, and he was beginning to suspect she would do it for him, too. She was taking lunch to school for his son, and it felt like the most personal step the two of them had taken since she moved back. Except, perhaps, for the kiss she'd given him for not letting her dad get washed off the ferry in the storm.

"I won't leave without you," he said. "So don't rush."

Maddox watched Camille drive away in his truck, and the heavy weight of being a single parent eased for a moment. He turned back to loading the ferry and welcoming his passengers, knowing that no matter what the future brought for him and Camille, they seemed to have finally eased the sting of the past.

CAMILLE SHOOK HANDS with the real estate agent and promised him a definite answer within the month, even though, in her heart, she was determined. She couldn't keep making candy on the island and hauling it across the lake. It was time-consuming and cumbersome. Having a warehouse building on the very end of the row of shops in Lakeside was a double benefit, because she could remodel the front as a store and have a combined kitchen and store, just like they did on the island. All she needed was the courage to sign the paperwork and an awning that matched the store on Christmas Island. She'd done the math, and she believed another store would only expand their original business, not compete with it.

She also needed to tell her family the new phase of her plan. She suspected Cara already knew, because her younger sister had been paying attention when Camille talked about how convenient it would be to manufacture in Lakeside and not just use the rented building as a warehouse and distribution facility. Cara had even made the trip with her a few times.

Distribution was one thing, but would her parents be shocked that she might set up an actual store and divide her time? With half the business on the mainland and the possibility for a year-round storefront, Camille could even consider getting an apartment in Lakeside. Did she need to be on Christmas Island to run Island Candy and Fudge?

"Ready to go?" Maddox asked, coming through the door just as the Realtor, Mac Larson, left.

"Almost," Camille said. "One minute."

She spun in a slow circle, imagining how the empty building could be transformed into a modern candy kitchen with glass windows where visitors could watch sugar being pulled and fudge being boiled. Would such a store draw customers all year long? It would be a gamble, but so was coming home to the island.

It had been a gamble asking Maddox to use the golf cart he kept at the dock in Lakeside to pick her up. She'd dropped off his son's lunch, and thankfully the school secretary, Ruth, didn't ask any awkward questions. She'd been there throughout Camille's years in school and knew everyone.

"I still have to return the truck," she said. "The rental place is about a mile outside town."

"I don't mind following you. I'm hanging around here until you're ready to make the return trip. I already have the mail and packages stowed safely on the ferry, so now I just need you."

Camille glanced over at him as he leaned in the door frame of her rented building. He needed her?

"You're my only passenger," he explained.

"Oh," she said. "Then I better stop holding you up. The shipper picked up ten minutes ago, so my work is done."

"I noticed Mac Larson leaving as I came in," Maddox said.

Camille swallowed. She'd imagined herself revealing her plan to her family, but she wasn't going to lie to Maddox, who would figure out on his own why she was talking to a real estate agent.

"Are you buying this building?" he asked.

"Thinking about it."

He nodded. "I'm investing in some property here in Lakeside, too, adjacent to the land we already own at the dock. Future expansion, the ferry terminal I told you about."

"Look at us, just a couple of kids from the island making it big," Camille said.

He laughed. "Don't count my chickens yet. I'm just hoping to make it to bedtime without any tears."

Camille locked the empty building and got in her truck. She drove slowly, giving Maddox the opportunity to keep up with her on the golf cart.

Once she'd returned the truck, she slid into the golf cart with Maddox.

"Almost forgot I need to make one stop downtown," he said.

"I'm at your mercy." Camille laughed.

"You don't mind?"

Camille put a hand on his arm. "I'm not in a hurry now that I've shipped off my candy and turned in my truck."

"Good. I need to get Ethan an extra pair of shoes and some socks. I don't know what he does to his socks, but I can only find three pairs right now, and two of the socks have a hole."

"Lost in the laundry?"

"Or under his bed or maybe crammed down into his snow boots."

"It's not easy, is it?" Camille asked. Seeing Maddox as a father, a responsible adult, was…different. Over the past seven years, in her mind she had viewed him as the impulsive teenager who had betrayed her love. Circumstances had forced him to change. If she let him deeper into her life now, would everything be different?

"I've been more the part-time parent in the past, but now that Ethan will be with me more of the time and his schooling is my responsibility, it makes you wake up and pay attention to every detail. No one else is going to come along and make sure he does his spelling homework and has clean clothes every day and clean sheets at least once a week."

"And lunch," Camille said.

Maddox sighed. "Sometimes I need a little help from a friend."

They stopped at a general store in Lakeside's shopping district, and Camille helped Maddox shop. It felt so…ordinary, but personal. She held up a pair of silly socks, knowing Maddox would laugh, predicting his exact expression. At the register, he pointed to the packaged chocolate bars and raised an eyebrow, because he knew she disapproved of cheaply produced candy.

When they returned to the ferry, Camille sat in the pilothouse where it was warm while she waited for Maddox to check the ferry's engine and systems and then join her in the pilothouse for the trip home.

She sat next to him as he set their familiar course across the lake. It was strange but comfortable. Maddox glanced over at her, and she could guess he was thinking the same thing. How had they gotten to this point where they could be comfortable again with each other, even friendly?

"I never imagined this happening," he said. "In all the years since...you know... I didn't think there would be a time in the future when we'd go shopping for socks together."

Camille laughed. "Me, neither."

"I've been afraid to ask all day, but has your sister changed her mind about calling off her wedding?"

"Not that I know of, but I haven't seen her since about midnight last night. She was cried out by then."

"What I said about ships having two captains—"

"Don't worry about it," Camille interrupted. "I have a backup plan in case Chloe decides to stay on the island and she wants to reclaim her spot at the store."

"Your Lakeside property."

Camille nodded.

"But that would be like letting Chloe drive you away from the island."

"I've been driven away before," Camille

said. She regretted her words as soon as she said them.

"I'm glad you came back," Maddox said, his voice low and serious.

"I am, too."

"Rebecca said something last night that made me realize what I'd never understood before, even though I should have," Maddox said.

Camille waited. Her friend had a way of seeing through to the heart of everything, a gift honed by a challenging childhood that had somehow left her openhearted and optimistic.

"She said you didn't want to be number two."

Camille turned and looked out the side windows of the pilothouse. How could Rebecca have told him something that personal? Cara was the only other person who knew how tough it had been for Camille to grow up comparing herself to Chloe. She believed she'd hidden it from everyone else. Knowing that Maddox knew her secret made her feel vulnerable.

"I doubt that anyone wants to be number two," she said lightly.

She felt his hand on her shoulder, his fingers warm and light. "I did that to you, too, when I cheated on you. I'm sorry."

Camille felt hot tears burn her eyes, and she didn't dare turn and let Maddox see her face. She'd never expected to have this conversation with him.

"It's all in the past," she said. "And you were right that I need to let it go."

"I think I indirectly caused a snowball fight with that statement."

Camille shrugged. "There were no serious injuries. And it was freeing."

A month or even a week ago, she might not have been able to be gracious about an apology from Maddox, but she'd felt something changing within her. Perhaps it was the realization that no one else could make her feel second-best without her permission. She'd given an old wound too much sway over her life. Had it held her back?

She opened the side door of the pilot-house and let the December air cool her cheeks as she walked down the narrow staircase. She was the only passenger on the ferry, so she chose a seat right in the middle and pulled her knees up to her chest. Camille focused on the blue water ahead of her and the island growing closer.

When the ferry approached the dock and Maddox sounded the horn, she stretched out her legs and walked off the ferry without a backward glance. Equating being cheated on with being a middle child wasn't the clean match Maddox seemed to believe it was. His words were well-meant, but there was still a gulf between them. As she left the dock, she thought she heard her name, but she didn't turn around. Putting herself first was empowering, but she had things to accomplish before she let Maddox get too deep under her skin.

CHAPTER NINETEEN

CAMILLE WALKED INTO her parents' kitchen on a Tuesday morning just ten days before Christmas. Her mom was leaning against the counter by the coffeepot, her dad was scrolling through the news on his phone with a half-eaten plate of toast in front of him and Cara was at the stovetop scrambling eggs. It was a happy, comfortable family scene, the kind Camille had missed while she was away and was missing now by choosing to live downtown in her own gray and quiet apartment. Not that she regretted that choice.

Choice. That was her word of the day. After her trip to Lakeside to deliver the final shipment of Christmas candy and meet with the Realtor, she was determined to make her own way in the family business, no matter what Chloe did or did not do about her wedding. Her talk with Maddox on the return trip only cemented what she knew in her heart.

She had to put herself first.

"I'm glad you're all here," she said as she walked in.

Her mother smiled at her. "We're almost all here. Chloe's still in bed."

"That's okay," Camille said. "I wanted to talk to you first anyway, so this is good."

"Sounds serious," her father commented. "Is everything okay?"

Camille nodded.

"Sit down and have some breakfast," Cara said. "I'll crack some more eggs."

"Thanks, but I don't want to talk with my mouth full."

"That never stops your mother," her dad said.

Camille's mom laughed and swatted him on the shoulder. "You love listening to me, remember?"

"What did you say?" he asked.

Camille smiled. Her parents had the kind of relationship she wanted. It seemed so easy, but they must have had tough times. Her mother wasn't from the island. Was it a difficult adjustment when they were first married, or even in the many years since, with his parents living on the island and Melinda's a ferry trip away until they passed on? Some people could make it work, so maybe Chloe and Dan would be all right.

Since spending the day with Maddox, Camille had begun to feel differently about him. When they were teens and had fallen in love, it had seemed just as easy as jumping into the lake or rolling down a grassy hill on a summer day. They'd been swept into it without really thinking about it, and it had been swept away from them just as easily. Now that they were both adults with their eyes open, was it possible there was a future for them? Her heart tugged her in his direction, and her mind had put on the brakes for the past six months. But would it be so dangerous to take her foot off the brakes?

Her family waited patiently, but Camille hesitated a moment before laying her big news at their feet. She took a deep breath.

"I want to tell all of you about the next step I want to take with our business."

"More change?" her mother asked. Her

tone wasn't confrontational—instead it sounded like worry. Camille knew all her pushing and prodding and expansion was tough on herself, but she was also dragging her family along for the ride.

She hesitated a moment, trying to think of how to soften the news, but it was better to just rip off the Band-Aid.

"You know I've been renting a building in Lakeside for distributing candy, but I'd also like to start producing it there so I don't have to keep driving that truck on and off the ferry. It's not efficient, and our online sales were such a success that clearly this is the direction our business needs to go."

Her father's expression was neutral, her mother's was kind but concerned and Cara didn't look surprised at all.

"And this means I'll be spending more time there." Camille swallowed. She might as well get it all on the table. "Eventually, I'd like to open a storefront there, too, and capitalize on the tourist trade on the mainland. This would expand our family business, and we'd all profit."

"You would use our name?" her father asked. "Our logo and recipes?"

Was he questioning her idea, or did he think she didn't have the right to do this? Had Camille misjudged her family's attitude toward expansion all along? Were her parents going to deny her the ability to take the business name and trademark and open a new branch?

"Yes, if I can."

The kitchen was silent for a moment while Camille felt quivers of worry run through her. For the first time in her life, she was putting herself and her dreams first. She wasn't reacting and running away from the island this time. No matter what Chloe did, whether she chose to stay on the island and claim her spot in the candy store or if she married Dan and moved off the island, Camille was taking a proactive step toward her own happiness. If her family didn't see that and support her decision, she would find another way.

"If you don't—" she began.

"That's a great idea," her father said. "I wish I'd had the courage to do it myself years ago."

Camille let out her breath. "Really?"

Her father stood up and took a step toward her. "You know our fudge recipe is the best one in the entire world. I stand by every single thing we make and sell. I've always wanted to expand, but I just couldn't see how to make it work with the business here and you three girls to take care of."

"We did talk about it once years ago," her mother said quietly. "But you have to make choices in life, and we chose to invest our time and energy into you and your sisters."

"But you're free to do this," her dad said. "You can make the investment we never could."

Camille thought of Maddox for a moment. She was free. Finally free of the pain from the past and the way he had hurt her. And free of feeling second best. She was the only person who could choose to put herself first.

"Will you move to the mainland?" Cara asked.

"Maybe," Camille said. "I haven't worked that out yet."

"You could make it a year-round business," Cara said. "And you've lived away from the island for a long time. So you know you can survive in the wild." She smiled. "And I can come over to Lakeside and work for you when I get tired of all the Christmas Island cheerfulness. A person can only take so much of that."

She gave Camille a huge hug, and then Camille's parents joined in. Camille felt as if this was truly the beginning of her life. Unlike her departure seven years ago, she was putting herself and her dreams first. She was going to—

"What's all the hugging about?" Chloe's voice came from the door. "You haven't even heard my good news yet."

The group separated, and they all turned to see Chloe in the door looking pink and fresh. "I'm getting married in eight days."

Cara cut Camille a sympathetic look, and Camille knew exactly what she was thinking. Upstaged, again, by Chloe. Always. Story of her life. *Their* lives. There was no way to dislike Chloe, and Camille and Cara loved her for her openhearted sweetness despite her apparent perfection. Chloe's re-

cent waffling and soul-searching about her
dream wedding had shown the entire family that Chloe was, mercifully, not perfect.
Watching her struggle and doubt herself
was, Camille suddenly realized, part of her
own catharsis.

Camille smiled at her younger sister to
let her know that it no longer bothered her,
and then she turned and opened her arms
to Chloe to be the first to congratulate her.

MADDOX TOOK ADVANTAGE of a dry, sunny
day and set up a ladder in front of his hotel.
The place was mostly closed for the season. They'd offer dinner and drinks a few
nights a week for locals and host a small
Christmas party, but this was the time of
year when he could get some work done
around the place, weather permitting.

The gutter on the front corner tended to
drip and create a puddle on the sidewalk,
and that puddle was solid ice all winter. Before someone took an ugly fall, he needed
to get to the source of the problem. Maddox
climbed up twelve feet and took a screw-
driver from his pocket to pry off the mesh
cover. As he worked, he saw Camille com-

ing down the street. No, *bouncing* down the street was a more apt description.

He'd thought a lot about Camille. She had existed in his mind as his true love and the one who got away. For seven long years, he had kicked himself for what he'd done and for what he'd ruined. He was over that. He'd apologized to her, he'd pledged his love and time to his son, and he was going to build his family business. It was the future that mattered.

And maybe that future could involve a pleasant friendship with Camille. He'd begun to hope there could be something more between them and that the love they had once shared had not entirely died out, but he was an adult now, no longer impulsive. He could take his feelings and box them up, just as he had done before, especially if she was serious about moving away from the island. He knew from bitter experience that there was no way to exist in both worlds with one person tied to Christmas Island and the other across the lake.

"Hello," Camille called from below the ladder.

"Careful," Maddox said. "There's an icy patch on the sidewalk."

"I know. It's been there for a month."

"Working on it," he said. He peeled off a strip of dried-up old caulk.

"How's everything going?" she asked.

"I should ask you that. You seem as if your feet aren't touching the ground. Maybe I should have you float up here and fix this gutter for me."

"It's a sunny day," she said.

"And?"

"And Chloe's wedding is back on. December 23 in the island church, just as planned."

"What made her change her mind?" The last he'd seen her, Chloe was leaving the community Christmas sing-along in tears after putting her fiancé on the ferry.

"Would you believe wisdom and maturity?"

Maddox laughed. "When it comes to love, those things aren't always involved." He knew he was taking a risk by saying it, but he needed to be honest with Camille. There was no other way for them to move on.

Camille smiled. "Either Chloe realized she was never going to find anyone as perfect as Dan—"

"Despite the fact that he doesn't like water or ferries and she loves island life," Maddox interjected.

"Definite issues," Camille said. "But he's willing to fly, and she's decided she's willing to take a chance on mainland living for love. Even though I think they'll spend as much time on the island as they can."

Maddox smiled down at Camille. "I'm glad for her and Dan. And for you, too, right?"

"Me?"

"Well, with Chloe leaving, that means you lose one captain."

Camille's expression shifted from sunny to partly cloudy. "I was working around that."

"With your mainland property purchase." She nodded.

Maddox came down the ladder. "But will you go through with that now? If Chloe is leaving, then shouldn't you stay here and take charge of the business?"

Partly cloudy turned to a threat of rain, and Camille's eyes narrowed slightly. "Chloe calling off her wedding wasn't my reason for wanting to expand our business. I was doing that for me. I was doing that because my changes so far have been very successful. I'd be a fool not to build on that."

He nodded slowly. "I see."

"Chloe can do whatever she wants, and so can I. My parents can keep this business here going just as they've always done, and I'll go to Lakeside and manage the branch location and all the online business."

"Have you told your family all this?"

"I just did. They were excited about it, and my dad even told me he wished he'd had the courage to do this a long time ago."

"Your dad has plenty of courage," Maddox said. "I doubt that was what kept him from doing it."

Camille looked away for a moment. "He said he chose to put his family first."

"I can understand that."

Camille swallowed. "And then my sister came in and sucked up all the attention in the room with her announcement about her wedding."

Maddox smiled sympathetically. "Nothing new there."

"It's okay. For the first time, it really didn't bother me." Her expression was a bunch of helium-filled balloons again. This was what was lightening her step, he realized. Being free of her number-two complex. It wasn't her feelings for him, obviously, because she was committed to leaving now.

"So you'll move away from the island," he said, trying for a neutral tone.

"If necessary, yes."

"Again," he said quietly.

Camille crossed her arms. "You act as if Lakeside is on another planet when you obviously know it's a short ferry ride away."

"Twenty-two minutes, give or take, depending on the wind." Maddox felt as if he was standing on the shore of the island feeling the rocks roll under his feet with the movement of the waves. Where was this conversation going? Just when he'd finally put his guilt to rest and decided there could be a future of friendship and possibly more with Camille, she was changing the whole game.

"See? Lakeside's right there." She pointed down Holly Street, where the ferry was tied up and the mainland was on the horizon.

"It's not as easy as you might think, managing to hold on to ties on both sides of the lake and trying to keep relationships in both locations," he said.

Camille's expression softened. "You know this from experience."

"Bad experience, yes. No matter how it started, I tried to make my marriage to Jennifer work. I tried to help run the ferry line and be a decent husband and father. I cleaned the gutters in our house in Lakeside and took out the trash early in the morning on my way to the dock. I thought I was giving it the effort it deserved."

"That must have been hard."

"No matter how hard I tried, and I learned a lot about myself from trying and failing, believe me. No matter how hard I tried," he repeated, "it didn't work. I know now why not."

"Why not?"

"I think you know very well why it didn't work," he said. Was Camille going to make him admit he'd never been able to love Jennifer? Wouldn't that be the ultimate insult to Camille, that he'd chosen Jennifer over her even though his feelings weren't strong?

"You didn't love her," Camille said sadly.

He shook his head. "I thought I was doing what was right, but I have a much clearer picture of what doing the right thing looks like now."

Camille's expression brightened, and Maddox wished he could see the lit pathway out of this conversation. There was no longer anything he could do about Jennifer. He was glad she'd found someone to move on with who truly loved her. He couldn't read Camille's mind about their future relationship, and maybe it wouldn't matter, either, because she was leaving the island. Again. There was only one thing that mattered in his life.

"Doing what is best for Ethan is the only thing that matters to me now. His happiness, a stable life and a magical childhood spent on this island—" he pointed to the ground as he emphasized the words *this island* "—are the reason I get up in the morning and the reason I work hard."

"Your son is what matters most," Camille said, a statement and not a question. Didn't she wonder if there was room for someone else? If so, why was she so determined to leave?

"It has to be that way," he said. He put a foot on the lowest rung of the ladder. "It helps me keep my priorities straight."

Camille opened her mouth to say something and then closed it again. Maddox felt his heart twist. Wanting a future with Camille couldn't come at the cost of jerking his son around. He couldn't bring her into their lives and then not have it work out. Ethan had already been through that once at his young age. It was better for Ethan if Camille remained nothing more than the candy lady.

As Ethan's father, it was Maddox's job to protect his son's heart, even if that meant denying his own.

Camille stepped carefully around the patch of ice and walked down the street. She paused under the awning of the candy store and looked back, but then she slipped inside and Maddox put his head down on the cold steel rung of the ladder. He was doing the right thing for all of them.

CHAPTER TWENTY

THE CANDY STORE was closed, but Camille planned to begin taking orders for Valentine's Day as soon as Christmas and the new year were past. She had an agreement worked out with the island airport to ship during January and February. It was more expensive than the ferry, and she couldn't move as many pounds and boxes of candy, but it was a way to keep the company's name out there until she could set up her facility on the mainland and ship in volume all year.

Instead of fudge on the wide marble tables, Camille and Cara worked with huge spools of wired ribbon in red, white and green. The island church only had forty pews, twenty down each side, but each of them needed a perfect bow. And perfect bows were harder to make than complicated spun-sugar candy.

"I know it's only three days until Chloe's wedding and these bows are really important, but there's fresh snow and my horses need exercise," Cara told Camille.

"You're not abandoning me."

"But they're restless. And it's not freezing today. Think how much the horses would like to get out there."

"I'd like a break, too," Camille said.

"See? It's a great idea."

"But this is our assignment. Remember, we chose this instead of making centerpieces for the reception," Camille reminded her sister.

"I thought we were getting a good deal until I had to make one of these. I won't be gone long, and I promise to do my part when I get back. Save my share for me."

Camille smiled at Cara. "Fine. I'll set these bows aside for a while and work on the cake topper. That's more my thing."

The wedding cake would serve two hundred guests, because nearly every year-round resident of the island was invited, as were thirty of Dan's family and friends, who were flying in and staying at the only hotel open during the winter—Maddox and

Griffin's. Chloe and Dan had planned a reception in Lakeside for later in the spring for all the guests not brave enough or able to fly over to the island two days before Christmas.

Camille and Cara had designed the cake using their years of experience with sugar. Three tiers covered in white fondant with Christmas trees made of spun sugar decorating the sides of the layers. There were also glistening snowflakes made of sparkling sugar. Camille had a large snowflake in a sugar mold that she would decorate and place on top of the cake along with fresh red roses.

Camille went to the candy counter and carefully opened the sugar mold, holding her breath that this snowflake would come out perfectly. It was her second attempt with the intricate pattern. Part of the snowflake had broken off on her first try, but she knew to be more careful this time. Even if this one turned out perfectly, she was going to make one or even two backups, just in case. Nothing was going to ruin her sister's wedding.

Sunlight streamed through the front windows as she turned out a perfectly formed sugar snowflake and laid it gently on a piece of parchment paper. She sighed with happiness. Things were going to be fine. Chloe would get married. Island Candy and Fudge would continue as always with its island store, and she would have her own project getting her Lakeside facility running. She might even open the store before the summer tourists arrived.

The shop was quiet except for the occasional creak from the century-old building. How much fudge had gone through the front door? A wave of nostalgia hit her. Did she really need to expand beyond Christmas Island and split her time with the mainland or, more extreme yet, move to Lakeside to live? What was wrong with keeping things as they were?

The glint of silver caught her eye on the street, and she looked through the front windows and saw Cara with two horses hitched to a sleigh. Cara stopped in the street and waved.

"What are you doing?" Camille asked as she opened the front door of the candy store.

"Exercising the horses and having some fun. Isn't that why we love this island?"

Camille laughed. Her younger sister was right. If it weren't for the perks of being able to drive a horse-drawn sleigh right down the main street of the town on a weekday afternoon, putting up with the hassles and isolation of a winter on the island wouldn't be much fun. Camille held up one finger. "Wait for me."

She dashed inside for her coat, hat and gloves and took one long look at the sugar snowflake that would adorn Chloe's wedding cake. Life on the island was nearly perfect on some days.

When she got out to the sleigh, Camille discovered she wasn't the only one who'd noticed the horses and bells. Ethan was tugging his dad by the hand and waving like mad to Cara with his free hand.

"Should we invite them?" Cara whispered to Camille.

"Of course."

"Okay. I didn't know where you and Maddox were right now."

"We're in the same place we've been for months and probably always will be."

"And where's that?" Cara asked.

"We're just friends," Camille whispered.

She looked up, smiled at Maddox and held out a hand for Ethan. "Are you riding forward or backward?"

"Forward," his dad answered for him. "I like to see what's coming."

Maddox and Ethan took the forward-facing seat in the antique sleigh. Although it was old, it was light, and its runners were solid. Cara had put some horse blankets on the seats as cushions and an extra blanket for warmth. Camille hesitated before climbing up into the seat across from Maddox and his son.

"Come sit with us," Ethan said, pointing to the empty place next to him. "We'll share the blanket."

Camille exchanged a glance with Cara, who was observing the whole social interaction.

"I don't want to crowd you," Camille said.

"You won't," Ethan insisted.

Camille complied, and Ethan put the blanket over her knees so all three of them sat cozily together. Camille appreciated the sweet thoughtfulness of the boy, but she noticed that Maddox had not said a word. If he'd meant what he said about his belief that off-island and on-island relationships never worked, he was clearly not thinking about rekindling their long-ago romance. He was devoted to his son and the island.

Would he turn her down if she offered? Had she been misreading his attentions earlier in the fall, or had his view changed?

The sleigh moved forward, and Cara turned away from her thoughts. She was the one who had held Maddox at arm's length for months, even after she'd felt her anger toward him start to melt. She wasn't angry anymore and hadn't been for a while. But where did that leave them?

Cara drove through downtown and along the lake road. Camille saw the Great Island Hotel up on the bluff. It was closed for the season, but it was still majestic. She thought about Thanksgiving night on the lawn as the trees were illuminated, when she had told Maddox there would be no starting over for them. Only a month had gone by, but time seemed to move at a different pace on the island.

The sleigh slowed, and Ethan bounced

up next to her, standing and pointing to the Winter Palace. "There's Uncle Griffin's house!" he said. He turned to Camille. "I get to go there on Christmas after I open my presents from Santa, and there will be more presents."

Camille laughed. Ethan's shining eyes were so sweet and innocent. She remembered Christmas morning when she and her sisters were little and they'd hurried to see what was under the tree.

"You should come, too," Ethan said. He put both hands on her legs and turned his earnest expression up to her. "You could bring candy."

Maddox put an arm around his son and pulled him back into place on the seat between the two adults. "She has her own family to spend Christmas with. And there will be plenty of sweet things to eat at Uncle Griffin and Aunt Rebecca's."

Camille knew Maddox was right, of course, but somehow his words made her feel uninvited. Left out of his life and Ethan's. Even though she had made no effort to be included, it hurt.

"Maybe next year," Ethan said cheerfully.

Maddox didn't look at Camille. Instead, he pulled his son closer and stared out at the cold, wind-tossed lake. Camille shivered as they passed several island homes on the lake road, and then Cara slowed to turn onto a crossroad that would take them on a loop through the center of the island and back to downtown.

As Cara gave the horses a command, the motion jolted Camille as much as her sudden realization that even if she decided she wanted him back, Maddox might not be there for the taking.

THE CHRISTMAS SEASON was turning out to be busier than Maddox and Griffin's previous year. Now that their hotel was almost completely renovated and had a full-service restaurant, they were the only game in town. After all, the Great Island Hotel was only open for special occasions in the winter. Keeping the massive, historic hotel on the hill open with its five-hundred-guest capacity wasn't cost-effective, but the smaller boutique-style hotel owned by the

May brothers could turn a decent profit while also providing a service to Christmas Island.

"Ready for this?" Rebecca asked him as they finished tying an extra strand of lights to the front porch railing to light the way for their party guests. "Griffin and I started to talk about winter profitability, but then we set it aside until you were available."

"I'm in favor of the idea," Maddox said. "The wedding in a few days is going to fill us to capacity. Maybe we should start offering winter wedding packages."

"I love that," Rebecca said. "What would be more romantic than a winter wedding on Christmas Island?" Her eyes shone with excitement, and Maddox imagined it wouldn't be long before he was helping plan his own brother's wedding. He remembered Griffin standing up for him as his best man seven years earlier, even though his parents and brother had been skeptical about it. After his divorce, he'd been sure he'd never put himself through another marriage. And he'd believed it was the best thing for his son, too, if he remained unattached and devoted to the boy, especially since his mother was getting remarried.

"Party time," Rebecca said. She ducked inside, where the restaurant was already set up for the Chamber of Commerce holiday party. Everyone who owned a business on the island was invited, from the airport owners to the couple who did bike rentals. They would each bring a guest. The Peterson family should be there, although Maddox hadn't seen the RSVP list, just the number. Fifty guests.

He lingered on the porch, enjoying the crisp winter air's contrast to the heat and light inside. Holiday fragrances emanated from candles and pine inside, but on the hotel's front porch, the air was fresh and clear. He'd flown with Ethan to the mainland earlier in the day and handed him over to his grandparents, who would spoil their only grandson and make sure he got to his mother's wedding in his rented tux the next day. Maddox would pick him up in a couple of days, catching a late plane after Chloe's wedding to get to the mainland and pick up both his son and Aunt Flora.

Maddox had a few days off from parenthood, and he couldn't decide if he was relieved or disappointed. He wasn't worried about his son's safety or happiness, but he'd grown so accustomed to listening for Ethan in the night and double-checking his homework and making sure he ate something decent that it would be strange and lonely.

A figure crossed the street. Camille. Her blond hair shone in the holiday lights, and she lifted her face to his as she stepped onto the sidewalk in front of the Island Hotel.

"Merry Christmas, Maddox," she said.

"Happy winter solstice," he said. "I like this day."

She nodded. "The longest night of the year. I remember going to the Winter Palace for Flora's birthday parties when I was a kid."

"Me, too. My brother and I are thinking of reviving that tradition next year in her honor, but this year the twenty-first happened to fall on the night of the chamber's party. We plan to go back and light some luminaries and drink a toast to Aunt Flora later."

"That sounds fun."

"Ethan's on the mainland getting ready for his mother's wedding, so I can stay out as late as I want tonight," Maddox said. He didn't mean for it to sound like an invitation. What would Camille say if he invited her back to the mansion after the party? Rebecca would be there. It would just be the four of them, two couples, so comfortable and too easy.

Even if she still loved him, even enough for a spark that could grow back into a flame, Camille was likely to leave the island, even if her older sister also left and there was no competition for running the family business. He would be foolish to risk his heart on the hopes she would change her mind when she clearly had bigger plans for her life. Maddox had big plans, too, but they all involved making his permanent home on Christmas Island, where his son would have the childhood he deserved.

In the crisp night air, the Christmas gift he'd impulsively purchased for Camille earlier that day seemed like a mistake, something born from the hope of the season instead of the reality. Should he tell Camille tonight? What did he hope to accomplish with the gift, and how would she view it?

"I remember coming to the chamber party a few times, too," Camille said, her voice wistful. "Sometimes my mom and dad would go together, and sometimes they'd bring me or one of my sisters."

"We danced together once," he said. "Before we were dating, when we were just two island kids going to a party with their parents."

Camille looked away. "We could dance tonight, since we're still two island kids."

Did she really want to dance with him? Was it just to prove that she'd moved past any hard feelings? Maybe he was part of her plan to shed the past and free herself of her issue with coming in second. She seemed to be over the Chloe thing, and dancing with him might prove to herself she was beyond caring about their past, too. He would dance with her, but he needed to remember that it meant nothing. There was no future for them.

"It's cold out here," Camille said, moving up the stairs and pausing next to him on the porch. "And I'm looking forward to the hot cider mentioned on the invitation."

"Is the rest of your family coming tonight? I know Chloe is pretty attached to the island, so I thought she might like the chance to come to the annual Christmas party one more time."

Camille shook her head. "The wedding is the day after tomorrow, and even Chloe has her limits when it comes to social events. I think Cara was torn between staying home and enduring wedding-prep mode or wearing high heels to a party where she'd be forced to make small talk with people she's known all her life. My mother won her over by giving her the job of writing out all the place cards for the reception, because she has the gift of gorgeous handwriting."

"Will they save some work for you?" Maddox asked.

"I'm making the wedding cake tomorrow. I have the gift of making beautiful things out of sugar."

"You have plenty of gifts."

They stood together in the darkness, lit only by holiday lights. Music and laughter wafted out to them from inside the hotel. Whatever their futures held, Maddox would always remember the moment with soft light reflecting off Camille's hair. They would at least have tonight.

He held out an arm. "Let's go inside and represent two island dynasties, past and future."

Camille laughed and took his arm lightly. They walked into the hotel, and Camille gave his arm a little squeeze before she cut across the room to where her friend Rebecca was talking to Mike, who owned the island bike rental.

Maddox checked in with Shirley from the Chamber of Commerce to make sure she was happy with the food, drinks and table arrangement. She had a small presentation planned for partway through the evening acknowledging some business highlights from the past season. Maddox had already seen the awards. The Kite

Shop was receiving an award celebrating its twenty-five years in business, and the Great Island Hotel had earned a community service award for sending its gardeners to maintain all the flower baskets downtown throughout the summer season. He imagined his ferry service and Camille's candy business would receive awards at next year's Christmas party for their major expansions, which would, hopefully, be complete by then.

Was this how it would be? Meeting up with Camille at random island functions and dancing with her once a year at the Chamber of Commerce Christmas party? He tried to swallow and found it hard. Was he really afraid to take a chance on her just because she might divide her time between the island and Lakeside?

Maddox stood next to the hot chocolate table, and the sweet aroma reminded him of his son, who would drink a gallon of hot chocolate every day if he was allowed to. Putting his son first in his heart and his plans was the only thing he could do.

Rebecca moved to the piano and began playing a classical piece along with a violin and cello player from the Great Island Hotel's orchestra, who were furloughed for the winter but stayed on the island each year anyway. Next, the trio began "Winter Wonderland," playing it slowly so it was just right for a slow dance. Two couples took to the small dance floor created near the musicians, and when Maddox glanced over to Camille, she was looking at him.

He stepped deliberately past tables of people he knew well as he kept his eyes only on her. One dance would put any romantic ideas to rest. They could be friends, and he was about to prove it.

He held out a hand, and she took it. They walked to the center of the dance floor, and Maddox put an arm around her waist as she put her free hand on his chest, right over his heart. Could she feel it beating? They had shared a hug the night of the boat rescue and then an impulsive kiss a few nights after that, but this deliberate joining of their hands seemed like so much more.

Maddox was afraid to breathe in her scent of peppermint and vanilla, because he was afraid the fragrance would swirl right to his heart and he'd never be able to let her go. She felt so right in his arms that it was almost as if they were seventeen again, innocent and in love, before mistakes defined them and the world intruded with its demands. He watched her face, wondering if she felt those memories, too.

Her cheeks were pink, her eyes bright. She stumbled over his foot, and he caught her, the action bringing her mouth close to his in a moment that seemed to last forever. They were seconds from kissing, and he didn't care that the eyes of the room were on them. He didn't care that she might leave the island and break his heart. All he wanted was to be in love with Camille and know she felt the same.

"This is a mistake," she said, drawing back from him. She dropped his hand and shook her head so slightly that only he was likely to notice in the crowded room with voices and music all around them.

Camille broke away from him and walked over to a group of shop owners, including her friend Violet. He noticed her chatting pleasantly with them, but she did not turn and look at him. Just when he was willing to take a chance and risk his feelings and his son's heart and affection, Camille had shut him down.

Maybe it was for the best, because he'd been on the very brink of risking everything.

CHAPTER TWENTY-ONE

CAMILLE WALKED INTO Chloe's pink bedroom the night before her wedding. Chloe was sitting on her bed, looking through a shoebox filled with pictures, papers, a necklace, athletic award ribbons and some dried flowers. She smiled.

"I have one of those boxes, too," she said.

Chloe looked up. "No, you don't. You're not sentimental."

"Wait," Camille said, holding up one finger. She went across the hall and dropped to her knees next to her bed. She lifted up the bed skirt and reached into the darkness for the box she hoped was still there. Her fingers found dusty cardboard, and she slid the box out and carried it to her sister's room. She set it next to Chloe's box on the bed. "Told you I had one."

"What's in it?"

"I'm afraid to even look," Camille said.

"Most of it is at least ten years old, and I don't remember what's in here."

She lifted the lid and set it aside. A picture of her and her two sisters from Chloe's graduation was on top. Chloe wore a red cap and gown with a green tassel, the school's colors matching the island's theme, and Cara and Camille both wore pastel dresses, Cara's pink and Camille's mint green.

"Look at us," Chloe said, picking up the picture. "We were so pretty. What else is in there?"

Camille pulled out a ribbon from the Holiday Hustle from the year she and Chloe had come in second place in the island-wide race to celebrate Christmas in July. "That was so much fun," Camille said. "We should make it a tradition to get at least two candy girl sisters together every summer to compete."

"Oh, for pity's sake. Are you two getting all mushy with your shoeboxes of memories?" Cara stood in the doorway, arms crossed but a smile on her face.

"Join the party," Camille said. "Bring your box of treasures from under your bed."

"Very funny," Cara said. "What makes you think I have one?"

Camille looked at Chloe and grinned. "Should we search her room?"

"Better yet," Cara said, "I'll indulge you by looking at your old pictures and junk."

All three women sat cross-legged on Chloe's bed and plucked items from her memory box and Camille's.

"Oh, my goodness," Cara said, holding up a picture of Chloe's eighth birthday, when she got a bike. "Look how young Mom and Dad are in this picture."

Camille took a close look. "It was twenty years ago. What are we going to look like in twenty years?"

"Gorgeous, of course," Chloe said.

"I hope so," Camille said. She'd come into her sister's room for a reason, and she had to go through with it. It was now or never, since Chloe was getting married and leaving the next day. Camille put a hand on both her sisters' arms. "There's something serious I want to talk about, and I'm glad you're both here to hear it."

Both Cara and Chloe looked up from

the invitation to the Great Island Hotel's Christmas in July party.

"It's about our business," Camille said. "You know I'm planning to open a manufacturing and shipping center in Lakeside with, I hope, a storefront."

Both her sisters nodded.

"And I was thinking of dividing my time between our island store and the Lakeside one, possibly even moving to Lakeside part of the year to manage it."

Camille let out a breath. There would be no taking back what she was about to say, but it was time.

"I don't want to manage it all by myself," she said. "I need someone I can trust who is amazing at managing a candy operation to run the Lakeside kitchen and store."

Chloe's eyes widened, and Cara's mouth dropped open.

"Chloe, would you be my partner in Lakeside?"

"Oh, my gosh, are you serious?" Chloe asked.

Camille nodded.

"What a wonderful idea," Cara said, smiling at Camille, her expression like that of a proud parent watching a child take its first steps.

"And you really want me to run it?" Chloe asked. "Really?"

Camille reached out to her sister and hugged her. "Really."

"Dang it," Cara said.

Camille released her older sister and turned to her younger one. "What?"

"You're making me cry," Cara said.

"From happiness?" Camille asked.

"Pure joy. If you two are running both candy operations, we'll be rich and no one will notice if I slip out the back door of the candy shop on sunny days."

Chloe clutched Camille's arm. "I know you're doing this for me so it will be easier for me to move to Lakeside. I'll still feel connected to home this way. But I don't want you to do this if it's not really what you want."

"It's what I want," Camille said. "We can be equal partners and share the family business we both love."

"I'm so glad we can do this together," Chloe said.

"There's only one thing, though," Camille said. "You'll be running the distribution side, and it'll be busy all year long, I hope."

Chloe made a face of trepidation. "I hope I can handle it."

Camille smiled. "I know you can. Our future is in your hands while I kick back on Christmas Island."

The three sisters held hands and laughed, and when their parents came to Chloe's bedroom door to see what all the noise was about, Camille told them her plan.

"We love it," her father said.

"And you'll stay on the island," her mother said, beaming with happiness.

Camille nodded, and her eyes fell on the box open on the bed in front of her in which only a few items remained. One of them was a white daisy, its petals delicate but still intact.

CAMILLE FELT LIKE walking on tiptoes through her parents' house on the morning of December 23. The wedding was scheduled for noon, with a reception in the church hall immediately following. Later in the afternoon, the bride and groom would catch the eight-seater plane leaving the island just before dark.

Rebecca had told Camille that Maddox would also be on that plane to Lakeside so he could pick up Ethan and Flora Winter and return with them early on Christmas Eve. It seemed so strange that her ex-boyfriend would make the first short leg of the honeymoon trip with Camille's sister, but that was island life. There was only one plane leaving the island airport.

When Camille swung open the front door that led directly into the kitchen, she breathed a sigh of relief. Chloe, Cara and their parents were having a late breakfast, smiling and talking as if it was any day.

"I hope you saved some for me," Camille said. "I'm starving."

And she was. Camille had hardly eaten a thing since the Christmas party at the Island Hotel. She kept thinking about that dance with Maddox. That moment when she'd been off balance and he'd held her close, her lips nearly brushing his. Never in her life had she wanted to do something so badly as she'd wanted to kiss him.

She'd broken away without explanation

because she didn't want to tell him that she was falling in love with him all over again just when it was too late. He'd drawn back from her, almost a reversal of their roles from earlier in the fall. Had she waited too long? She was afraid to say what was in her heart and show that much vulnerability. She was afraid of being rejected.

As she'd chatted with friends until she thought she could leave without raising eyebrows, she'd felt his gaze on her, but she hadn't dared look at him. Instead, she'd spent the entire previous day making an ornate wedding cake for her sister, complete with glittering snowflakes and Christmas trees on a landscape of snow-white fondant.

"We have plenty," her mother said. "I made a feast because I know how wedding receptions go. By the time you talk to everyone and do all the formalities like cutting the cake, it seems like you hardly eat a thing."

Camille took her seat at the family table, the same seat she'd occupied growing up. Everyone was in their usual spot, and Camille took a moment to look around the table at the people she loved most in the world. After today, with Chloe leaving the nest, would things ever be the same again?

"No crying," Chloe said, smiling at her. "I'm an expert at this, and I think you were just about to let those tears roll."

Camille laughed. "Sorry. I was getting all sentimental there."

Chloe fanned her face. "Stop. I already did my eye makeup, and I'm only thinking happy thoughts until after the pictures."

"What planet is this?" their dad asked. "Have my girls switched places?"

Two hours later, as Camille lined up with her sisters and their father in the back of the church, she remembered that moment at breakfast and smiled. She would never switch places and be the gushy, sentimental person Chloe was, but there were elements of that sentimentality she liked. Chloe loved deeply and passionately. She wasn't afraid to say what was on her mind, no matter how vulnerable it made her. And she'd made the bold choice of falling in love and getting married, despite her worries.

Her father carefully brought Chloe's veil over her face and took her arm. The expression on Chloe's face told Camille everything she needed to know about love. It was worth it.

With that thought in her mind, she counted to eight as instructed and then walked slowly down the aisle behind her sister Cara. She saw Dan waiting at the altar. She glanced to her left, where she saw Dan's friends and relatives, who were mostly strangers to her. On her right were the Christmas Islanders—Violet, Jordan, Mike, Hadley, Rebecca, Griffin.

And Maddox. He was tall like his brother, and he stood at the end of the pew, right on the aisle. His eyes bored into hers for a moment, and Camille considered tossing her bouquet aside and reaching out for him with both hands. What would he do if she told him she loved him right there in the aisle with the bride on her heels?

Instead, she smiled at him and held his eyes a moment longer than necessary for someone who was an old friend. He was more than that, but she didn't know how to describe it.

After the wedding, Camille dutifully posed for family and bridal party photos, smiling until her cheeks hurt. "Are we allowed to cry now?" she asked Chloe.

"Yes, but you know what? I don't feel like crying. I've never been happier, and I'm ready to dance at my party."

Camille's dad put an arm around her and led her toward the reception hall. "You just never know, do you?" he asked.

"It must be true love," Camille said.

"That's what your mother said. And I'm so proud of you for asking Chloe to run half of the business. I used to think you didn't like playing second fiddle to her, but I guess I was wrong, wasn't I?" He smiled at Camille, and they both laughed.

The reception was packed, and the noise of happy voices echoed from the walls. Camille did her ceremonial duties as a member of the bridal party while keeping an eye on Maddox. Would they have a chance to talk? The greatest risk would be to tell him she loved him. It was entirely possible he didn't feel that way and truly believed they were friends, just as he'd been saying.

And then there was the possibility that he loved her but feared their relationship would never work because she had plans that would take her away from the island he'd pledged to make his home. When she told him her plans had changed, what would he say?

The risk had to be taken or she would never know. She'd thought at one time that being cast aside by someone she loved was the worst thing that could happen to her, but now she wondered if it was worse to love in the face of great uncertainty.

There was a break in the music, but when it started again, Camille swept the room, looking for Maddox, and resolved to ask him to dance. She would suggest they finish what they had started at the Christmas party two nights ago. He was near the dessert table, talking to Jordan. Camille took three long steps, hurrying before she changed her mind.

"Father-daughter dance?" her dad asked as he stepped in front of her. "I never know when I'll get the chance to dance with all three of my beautiful daughters in one day."

She took one last look at Maddox, who hadn't even seemed to notice her moving his way, and then turned a gracious smile on her father. "I'd love to."

As she danced with her dad, the winter sun faded outside the windows. It wouldn't be long before the bride and groom made their exit. The song she was dancing to with her dad seemed to go on forever, and when she looked over to the dessert table, Maddox was gone.

Camille joined Rebecca and Griffin after the dance and quietly asked Rebecca where Maddox had gone. "Home," she said. "To change and grab an overnight bag. He's going straight to the airport to catch the plane."

MADDOX HAD NOT rushed over and asked Camille to dance. He needed to get accustomed to the idea that she was not likely to make the island her forever home and that the roller coaster they'd been on for a few months had to come to an end for everyone's sake—especially his. Camille had never made him any promises and had barely agreed to being friends. Was everything else in his imagination? A figment of

the happy reconciliation and future he believed would make him complete?

He was already complete. He'd forgiven
himself for his past mistakes. He had a
child who was pure sunshine. Camille had
passed on a chance to plaster him with a re-
venge snowball. He should be able to draw
a deep breath and move on.

As he drove to the airport, Maddox
passed familiar island landmarks, all of
them holding memories. Trails he'd biked
on with his brother and nearly gotten lost
on after dark on summer nights. Homes
of fellow islanders, rental houses vacant
for the winter. He negotiated a curve in
the dimming light and noticed the Peterson
family minivan right behind him, with the
father of the bride driving the newly married couple to the airport.

The island airport, on a flat hilltop in the
center of the island, came into view, and
a small plane was running and waiting at
the end of the runway.

Maddox parked his truck and then waited
by the plane as the bride and groom, still
wearing their wedding clothes, got out of
the van. Chloe kissed her father and then

took her new husband's hand and boarded the plane. Maddox watched the joy on their faces, and he knew the sad truth was that his own marriage had not begun with such radiant happiness. That level of joy had never come from his relationship with his wife, but he did have it with his son.

Maybe that would be enough.

They took their seats on the plane, and Chloe turned around to say hello to Maddox.

"I'm the luckiest person on earth," Chloe said. "I was so sad about leaving the island, but I'm taking a big piece of it with me."

"What's in your suitcase?" Maddox joked.

Chloe laughed. "I mean the candy business. Camille is planning to start a store and kitchen in Lakeside, and last night she asked me to be her partner and manage the Lakeside operation so she can stay on Christmas Island."

The plane lifted off from the runway and circled over downtown, where Christmas lights glowed, but Maddox felt as if he could fly without the help of the airplane. If Camille had asked Chloe to be her partner, it could only mean one thing—she had gotten over her feelings of being second in command, being in second place. What else had she let go?

"She'll run the flagship store on the island and manage our website and advertising, but I'll be over in Lakeside making the family recipes. It will almost feel like home," Chloe continued.

With Camille staying on Christmas Island, it would continue to feel like home to Maddox. He watched the lights disappear as they crossed the lake and prepared to land in Lakeside on the winter night. As much as he was looking forward to collecting his son and meeting Aunt Flora's driver to take them all to her home on the mainland, he would gladly have bailed out over the island just to ask Camille what was in her heart.

He sat back and took deep breaths, reviewing every look Camille had given him at the wedding ceremony and reception. Had she been waiting for an opportunity to tell him about her change of plans? Regret stabbed him in the gut. He should have asked her to dance, and now he had to fulfill his promises and pick up his son and Aunt Flora, no matter how much he wanted to rush back to Camille.

Asking the plane to turn around was something he would have done in the past, but he'd learned that being impulsive came at a cost, and if something was meant to be, it was worth waiting for. Even though the hours until he could return to Christmas Island loomed before him like an eternity.

CHAPTER TWENTY-TWO

CAMILLE ARRIVED AT the candy store early on Christmas Eve to start a fresh batch of chocolate-peppermint fudge. She already had chocolate-covered pretzels, coconut-covered white chocolate cake balls, peppermint bark and gingerbread cookies ready to go. All she needed to do was slice up fresh fudge and put together the care packages.

"I'm here," Cara said as she came through the front door, letting in a burst of frosty air and stomping snow off her boots. "Barely. It was a late night, to say the least."

Camille checked the candy thermometer on her batch of fudge as the aroma of chocolate permeated the air. "I can't believe Chloe is married and gone."

Cara laughed. "Not exactly gone. You put her in charge of half our candy empire, so she's not going far."

"Which is good, right?"

"It's actually great. I've always admired you, but when you gave Chloe a place in the family business even though she's leaving the island, I decided you were pretty darn amazing."

Camille smiled. "It was actually an obvious answer to all of our problems, but I just didn't see it until…"

"Until you realized you might not like leaving the island again?"

A tug of guilt brought down Camille's merry mood. "Do you think I'm being selfish?"

Cara stared at her a moment and then burst out laughing. "That is beyond ridiculous. You're saving us all from Chloe's angst about leaving, and you're probably going to make us millionaires by putting someone in charge of that new facility who really does know what she's doing."

"I know she does. She ran this business really well, and she seems enthusiastic about implementing my new ideas." She sat on the edge of a table and smiled at her younger sister. "Who would have thought daughter number two would be in the driver's seat?"

"Anyone who was paying attention," Cara said. "And I thought you'd finally hung up the whole middle-child complex."

"I've hung it out to dry for good," Camille said. "A few weeks ago, Maddox told me that a ship can have two captains, and now I finally see that he was right."

"I shouldn't ask this," Cara said. "But you know I want to."

"Does my decision to stay and run this store have anything to do with Maddox May?"

"Yep," Cara said.

Camille thought about her answer as she began to line up small red boxes along the countertop. Each box had a glittery gold design on the outside and was large enough to hold several pounds of Christmas treats. Cara followed her along the counter and laid a piece of green tissue paper in the bottom of each gift box. There were eighty of the gift boxes this year, one for each household that stayed on the island. Most of the families would send someone downtown at noon to pick up the package, as they always did, but Camille had a list of elderly island residents to whom she was planning to deliver the Christmas care packages that afternoon.

"I would miss all this," Camille said. "I've been missing it for seven years, even though I made it home for a few Christmases and helped a few times. Christmas Island is in my blood, and now that I've been back for six months, it would be so hard to leave. Plus, I've dragged our whole family into this big new venture. I have a responsibility to stay here on the island, where it all started."

"And you would miss me, right?" Cara asked.

Camille smiled. "I would totally miss you and your wisdom, even when you're telling me something I'm not ready to hear."

"Sorry about that."

Camille shook her head. "You were absolutely right. It's taken me some time to realize that I can let go of things and decide what luggage I'm going to haul with me."

"Is Maddox in your past or future luggage?"

"Both. And I'm finally at peace with that. I want to be here, and I know there's some kind of future for us. I just don't know what he's thinking right now."

"You're about to find out," Cara said, nodding toward the front window, where a silver pickup truck came to a stop on the street. Camille and Cara watched as Maddox, Ethan and Flora Winter got out of the truck and Maddox took Flora's arm and guided her toward the front door of the candy shop.

Camille and Cara opened the front door and greeted Flora, who pulled them both into a hug. "You Peterson girls are such beautiful young women now, and I heard all about Chloe's wedding from Maddox."

"It was wonderful," Camille said. She gave Maddox a questioning glance. She had known he was flying to pick up his son and Flora, but why were they stopping here? She tried to read his expression. He looked happy and relaxed. Was it the holidays? Having his son back? Spending time with his honorary aunt? His eyes stayed on Camille's face, and she smiled at him, hoping to convey that there was more than just holiday magic in the air.

"I came to see my house," Flora said.

"Maddox told me you recreated it in gingerbread."

"Oh, of course," Camille said. She pointed to the front window. "Let me turn on the lights so you get the full effect."

"I'll get the lights," Cara said, ducking inside.

"It's perfect, like a fairy castle," Flora said as she leaned close to the front window to admire the replica of the Winter Palace. "And what do I see on the chair on the balcony? Is that my beloved Cornelius?"

Camille laughed. "I hope I got the color of his fur right."

"It's just like him. I left him at home with my housekeeper since this is such a short trip, and it warms my heart to see him sitting there. What a wonderful summer we had this year."

The colored lights inside and around the gingerbread house lit up, and the Winter Palace glowed.

"I love it," Flora breathed. "It's never looked so good."

"Thank you. Now come inside and warm up," Camille said. "We're putting together our annual Christmas candy packages for the island residents."

"Do we get one?" Ethan asked.

Camille smiled at the boy and put a hand on his head. "Of course. You're an island resident now. The boxes aren't quite ready yet, but I'll make sure to save a perfect one for you and your dad."

"Do people still come and pick them up?" Flora asked. "I remember that so well as a child, but it was probably your grandfather I picked ours up from."

"The tradition lives on, just like everything else on Christmas Island," Camille said. She glanced at Maddox. "That's one reason why I love it here."

He raised both eyebrows as if he wanted to ask a question. Did he want to know all her reasons?

"I'm delivering some boxes this afternoon for our older residents," Camille said.

"Do you need any help?" Maddox asked. "Ethan is wrapping presents with Rebecca this afternoon at the Winter Palace. The roads are pretty snowy, and I have four-wheel drive on my truck."

"If you want to," Camille said.

"I do," he said quietly. He didn't reach out to touch her, but Camille felt the pull between them. "We've done it together before."

Instead of their past feeling like a pinprick, a stab of sorrow at what might have been, Camille remembered the two Christmases when she and Maddox had made the rounds together. Their last two years of high school, when life had seemed like an endless, happy, snow-covered road in front of them, and the aromas of peppermint and chocolate had filled the inside of their car as they'd driven around the island delivering joy.

"I remember," she said, smiling. "And I'd love your help."

"Can I come, too?" Ethan asked.

"Next year, buddy," Maddox said. "Aunt Rebecca really needs your help with presents today."

"Speaking of Rebecca, we should get going," Aunt Flora said. "I believe Griffin is anxiously waiting for the package we brought with us."

"A Christmas gift?" Camille asked.

Maddox nodded. "A big one. I'm sure you'll be hearing about it soon."

Flora smiled. "I've never seen my nephews so happy."

Camille noticed that she used the plural. Maddox did look happy, and he should. The ferry business was expanding, he had all the capital he needed and his son was with him all winter in their cozy home. Everything was going his way, but the way he looked at her as he walked out the door made her think she was also part of the happiness.

Cara finished the batch of fudge while Camille began filling the gift boxes. They put on some Christmas music, and Camille knew from the peace and joy she felt that she'd made the right decision to stay on Christmas Island. There would be long, gray winter days ahead, but nothing could dim her love for her home and the people who lived there. As Cara sliced the fudge, Camille's phone pinged.

"Is it Rebecca announcing an engagement?" Cara asked. "I'm guessing a ring is the special package Flora and Maddox brought back to give Griffin."

In answer, Camille walked over to her sister and showed her the picture she'd just received from her best friend. It was Rebecca and Griffin with their arms around each other, and Rebecca holding up her left hand, where a ring sparkled.

WE'RE GETTING MARRIED, the text below the picture said. AND FLORA BROUGHT A FAMILY HEIRLOOM RING!

Camille had never known her friend to use all capital letters before, but the situation definitely called for it.

Can't wait to see the ring. Congratulations!

Camille added three hearts and a smiley face and sent her message.

"People will start coming in to pick up their boxes soon," Cara said. "I'm happy to stay here while you and your man with the pickup truck go make the deliveries."

Camille grinned at her sister. "The roads are pretty snowy."

"And I want you to be safe and get the job done," Cara said.

They tucked treats into each box, wrapped them in clear cellophane and tied all eighty boxes with a length of red ribbon. Camille took fifteen of the gift boxes and set them aside for delivering. It was only moments later when she saw Maddox pull up out front.

"I'll be right back," Cara said. "I'm going across the street to Violet's to pick up my gift for Mom."

Cara ducked out the front door and passed Maddox as he came in.

"Did I scare your sister away?" he asked.

"Last-minute shopping."

Maddox took off his heavy coat and hung it over a chair. "I brought you a gift," he said, "but now I'm not sure it's the right thing."

Camille's heart thudded. He'd brought her something. She had something for him, too, tucked into her purse so she'd be ready.

"Why's that?" she asked. She stood by the long counter, and he closed the distance, striding over the black-and-white-checkered floor of the shop.

"On the plane yesterday, Chloe told us all about how she's going to handle your business in Lakeside and you're going to stay here on the island."

Camille nodded. "The night before her wedding, I asked her if she'd be willing. It seems like it'll make it a lot easier for her to move to the mainland if she still keeps the family connection."

"That was incredibly nice of you."

"And smart. Our ship has two captains now." She smiled and reached out and put her hand on his arm. "I was finally ready for that."

He moved closer. "I'm very glad you'll be staying here."

"Me, too."

"But it makes my Christmas gift seem a bit strange. I bought it three days ago when I thought you'd be either living in Lakeside or spending a lot of time there."

"Is it a ferry pass?"

He laughed. "Close. But you don't need a pass to ride my ferry. And when the lake is frozen during the winter, it wouldn't do you much good. I bought you a plane pass, good for unlimited rides for a year whenever the island air service is running."

Camille's heart hiccuped. "You bought it three days ago?"

He nodded. "I know I said that relationships separated by the lake don't work out, but I decided that trying is worth any risk. I bought the plane pass because I didn't want to stand in your way, but I wanted to let you know that I'm here for you anytime you want me."

Instead of answering, Camille stepped into his arms and held him tight. "That is the best gift anyone has ever gotten me."

"Even if it's useless now?"

She shook her head, scraping her cheek on his flannel shirt. "It's not useless. I'll have to fly over and help Chloe sometimes. Or just visit her. She's my big sister, but she might need my advice anyway."

She stayed in his arms, smelling his fresh lake scent and enjoying the feel of his warm hands on her back. She felt him kiss the top of her head, and then she tilted her head back and kissed him on the lips. It was warm and soft and took her back to the early days of their love. But it was something more than that, too. They were grown-up and had survived plenty of water under the bridge. Everything was different this time.

"Wait," she said, breaking the kiss. "I

have something for you, too." She went into the back room and retrieved the small present from her purse. "It's something useful but symbolic."

He took the gift and peeled back the green-and-white-striped paper and then removed the lid from the box, where a silver watch sat inside. "Is it waterproof?" he asked.

She nodded. "It's waterproof, and it has a compass right on the face, so you can find your way."

"Back to you?"

"If that's where you want to be."

He slipped on the watch and reached for her. "We've wasted a lot of time," he said.

"No," she protested. "It wasn't a waste. We're here now, and we both know what we want. That watch," she said, taking his hand and rubbing her finger around the edge of the watch face, "it only goes forward, not backward." She raised her eyes to his face. "I love you, Maddox, and all I can think about is spending my life with you on Christmas Island."

He took both her hands and kissed her again on the lips. "I love you, too, more than ever, and I want to spend every day with you."

"What do you think Ethan will say about this?"

Maddox laughed. "Are you kidding? He fell in love with you months ago when he saw you as the candy lady. Throughout the fall, he's started to think of you as one of the family. He even asked if he should call you Aunt Camille, like he calls your friend Aunt Rebecca."

"What did you say?"

"I said he could call you a candy girl instead."

Camille laughed. "You didn't."

He shook his head. "No. But we'll have to figure out together what he should call you. I want you to be part of our lives, Camille."

"I want that, too," she said. She kissed him for a long time, until she heard the shop door jingle.

"I'm sorry to interrupt, but people are going to start showing up for their Christmas boxes," Cara said. "And I didn't know if you wanted the whole island to know you're back together."

"That would be fine with me," Maddox said. He looked to Camille. "How about you?"

"They should get used to the idea," Camille said.

"Man, it's a lovefest this Christmas," Cara said, shaking her head. "I'm happy for you."

Camille beamed at her sister.

"But get out of here and deliver those holiday treats, will you?" Cara said.

Maddox laughed and walked over to the big crate filled with red-and-green boxes. He picked it up, and Camille held the front door for him. Then she let it snap closed behind them as they got in his truck to go deliver holiday joy to Christmas Island.

* * * * *

Get 4 FREE REWARDS!

We'll send you 2 FREE Books plus 2 FREE Mystery Gifts.

Love Inspired books feature uplifting stories where faith helps guide you through life's challenges and discover the promise of a new beginning.

FREE Value Over **$20**

HARLEQUIN SELECTS COLLECTION

19 FREE BOOKS IN ALL!

From Robyn Carr to RaeAnne Thayne to Linda Lael Miller and Sherryl Woods we promise (actually, GUARANTEE!) each author in the Harlequin Selects collection has seen their name on the *New York Times* or *USA TODAY* bestseller lists!

YES! Please send me the **Harlequin Selects Collection**. This collection begins with 3 FREE books and 2 FREE gifts in the first shipment. Along with my 3 free books, I'll also get 4 more books from the Harlequin Selects Collection, which I may either return and owe nothing or keep for the low price of $24.14 U.S./$28.82 CAN. each plus $2.99 U.S./$7.49 CAN. for shipping and handling per shipment*.If I decide to continue, I will get 6 or 7 more books (about once a month for 7 months) but will only need to pay for 4. That means 2 or 3 books in every shipment will be FREE! If I decide to keep the entire collection, I'll have paid for only 32 books because 19 were FREE! I understand that accepting the 3 free books and gifts places me under no obligation to buy anything. I can always return a shipment and cancel at any time. My free books and gifts are mine to keep no matter what I decide.

☐ 262 HCN 5576   ☐ 462 HCN 5576

Name (please print)

Address   Apt. #

City   State/Province   Zip/Postal Code

Mail to the **Harlequin Reader Service:**
IN U.S.A.: P.O. Box 1341, Buffalo, NY 14240-8531
IN CANADA: P.O. Box 603, Fort Erie, Ontario L2A 5X3

*Terms and prices subject to change without notice. Prices do not include sales taxes, which will be charged (if applicable) based on your state or country of residence. Canadian residents will be charged applicable taxes. Offer not valid in Quebec. All orders subject to approval. Credit or debit balances in a customer's account(s) may be offset by any other outstanding balance owed by or to the customer. Please allow 3 to 4 weeks for delivery. Offer available while quantities last. © 2020 Harlequin Enterprises ULC. ® and ™ are trademarks owned by Harlequin Enterprises ULC.

Your Privacy—Your information is being collected by Harlequin Enterprises ULC, operating as Harlequin Reader Service. To see how we collect and use this information visit https://corporate.harlequin.com/privacy-notice. From time to time we may also exchange your personal information with reputable third parties. If you wish to opt out of this sharing of your personal information, please visit www.readerservice.com/consumerschoice or call 1-800-873-8635. Notice to California Residents—Under California law, you have specific rights to control and access your data. For more information visit https://corporate.harlequin.com/california-privacy.

50BOOKHS22R

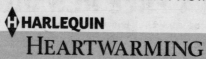
#411 A DEPUTY IN AMISH COUNTRY
Amish Country Haven • by Patricia Johns

Deputy Conrad Westhouse has one job—protect
Annabelle Richards until she can testify. The best place to
keep her safe is his ranch in Amish country, but getting to
know the beautiful witness means risking his heart...

#412 THE COWBOY MEETS HIS MATCH
The Mountain Monroes • by Melinda Curtis

Cowboy Rhett Diaz is starting an outdoor adventure company—
with needed help from Olivia Monroe's family. He just has to
get her across the country first... Can the road trip of a lifetime
lead to lifelong love?

#413 TO TRUST A COWBOY
The Cowboys of Garrison, Texas
by Sasha Summers

Hattie Carmichael's brother is marrying her childhood bully.
Participating in the hasty wedding is one thing—doing it alone
is another. Thankfully, Forrest Briscoe plays along with her fake
relationship ruse...until neither can tell what's real from pretend.

#414 SECOND CHANCE LOVE
Veterans' Road • by Cheryl Harper

Marcus Bryant returns home to Miami—and to old friend
Cassie Brooks. Their friendship never survived his joining the
air force after graduation. Planning their high school reunion
together might help them unravel the past...and find a future.
